"I think someone wants me and my daughter dead," Everleigh said.

Declan's jaw dropped in disbelief. He wasn't sure he'd heard correctly. "Excuse me?"

She handed him the note. Declan read it, then looked at her in confusion. It was threatening. "This is the first I've heard about a person seeking justice against a serial killer by going after his family members."

"So you don't think it's some sick joke?"

"It's possible," he responded. "Have you told anyone about your father?"

"No. It's not something I'd discuss—I'm actually disgusted by the idea of that killer having fathered me."

Declan was surprised how calm Everleigh appeared to be, although he suspected deep down that she was shaken.

"Detective, I came to see if you can help me find out who sent this letter to me," she said. "Someone wants me dead because of a man I've never met..."

Jacquelin Thomas is an award-winning, bestselling author with more than fifty-five books in print. When not writing, she is busy catching up on her reading, attending sporting events and spoiling her grandchildren. Jacquelin and her family live in North Carolina.

Books by Jacquelin Thomas

Love Inspired Cold Case

Evidence Uncovered
Cold Case Deceit

Harlequin Heartwarming

A Family for the Firefighter
Her Hometown Hero
Her Marine Hero
His Partnership Proposal
Twins for the Holidays

Visit the Author Profile page
at Harlequin.com for more titles.

VIGILANTE JUSTICE

JACQUELIN THOMAS

LOVE INSPIRED
INSPIRATIONAL ROMANCE

LOVE INSPIRED®
INSPIRATIONAL ROMANCE

Recycling programs
for this product may
not exist in your area.

ISBN-13: 978-1-335-46848-2

Vigilante Justice

Copyright © 2023 by Jacquelin Thomas

Love Inspired
22 Adelaide St. West, 41st Floor
Toronto, Ontario M5H 4E3, Canada
www.LoveInspired.com

Printed in U.S.A.

The fathers shall not be put to death
for the children, neither shall the children be
put to death for the fathers: every man
shall be put to death for his own sin.
—*Deuteronomy* 24:16

PROLOGUE

Legs planted wide and nostrils flaring, he stood on a hill, watching as a family gathered to lay their loved one to rest below him. His gaze was intense and unblinking. Sounds of people sobbing floated up to where he stood. He didn't know the deceased or any of the mourners. He didn't even care about them.

In this moment, it felt strange being here in Atlanta—he'd never wanted to come back to this place that was filled with nothing but bad memories.

"You okay?"

He had been too lost in thought to hear his brother's approach.

Pointing at the aging headstone, he said, "She's been dead thirty-two years today. I was six and you were only four."

"I know. I thought it was supposed to g-get easier with time. At least that's what people s-say."

"Yeah, that's what they say… They lied." A vein in his neck pulsed. "I can still remember that night. Begging her to let us stay home with her. She forced us to go with Dad. Said it was his weekend. Then coming home and finding her body…" She'd been bloodied and beaten. They'd been too young to know that she'd been raped, too.

"There wasn't anything we could've done. I b-barely remember wh-what happened. I only know what you told me." His brother spoke slowly to lessen his stutter, which grew worse when he was upset or anxious.

He gestured wildly in his anger. "Maybe not, but we could've tried to do something. You don't remember because I protected you from as much of it as I could." He had been tormented by guilt all these years, living each day with a dreadful sense of failure. It wasn't enough for the police to have found the man responsible for her death.

He recalled the day James Ray Powell was apprehended—three months after his mother's murder. It was all over the television. As they escorted the serial killer out to a waiting police car, he was laughing.

That's what I remember most. The laughing.

He drew in a few slow breaths to steady himself.

But the rage remained—it was a kind of cold fury that refused to leave. He'd never be rid of it until he dispensed the justice Powell deserved.

"Are we doing the right thing?" his brother asked.

"He took our mother away from us. We takin' his family from him. Tell me now if you're having second thoughts."

"N-naw…"

"Ya sure?"

"I'm good. Let's just get this d-done so I can focus on some other stuff. I've been thinking about my future. Got some plans in the works."

"Like what?"

Shrugging, his brother said, "I'm not ready to t-talk about it."

"Okay, whatever…" he said. "I found Ezra Stone. He don't live too far from here." He eyed his brother. "You with me on this, right?"

"Yeah. How m-many times I—I gotta reassure you. All we got is us."

They descended the hill, their steps muffled by the brown carpet of grass as they walked towards the faded yellow lines of the empty parking lot.

"Ride with me. I'll bring you back to your car."

They got into the car, started the engine and drove off.

They rode in silence for a while, the only sound coming from the radio playing hip hop music.

"You ever find out what happened to Pops?"

"Naw… It's pretty obvious that he abandoned us a long time ago."

"That ain't right," his brother said. "Something happened to him. His body just ain't been found."

"You can hang on to that dream, but the truth is that people out here don't care 'bout nothin' but they own lives. That's why we gotta take care of stuff ourselves."

When he glimpsed a police car a few vehicles behind them, he slowed down, cruising carefully down the street. He didn't want to risk getting a speeding ticket or even drawing attention to themselves.

Ten minutes later, he pulled into a parking spot near the corner. "That's the house right there."

They watched a man walk out of the house toward an old Cadillac. He unlocked the door and leaned inside. He appeared to be searching for something.

"That's him. Ezra Stone ain't changed a bit. Just got older."

"Old and gray," his brother responded. "He used to have m-more weight on him. At least that's how I remember him."

As he watched their target, he felt hot fury surge upward, threatening to explode.

Soon…

The thought of what they had planned appeased him. Temporarily. But his rage would return.

"We'll come back tonight," he announced.

"I'll be ready."

"It's time to make them all pay."

ONE

James Ray Powell is a cold-blooded killer. He stole the lives of so many women, leaving their families devastated and heartbroken. It is only right that he feels what we feel—the loss of a child, a wife, a mother, a sister... I won't stop until I erase every single member of that killer's family. This includes you and your daughter.

Everleigh Sanderson Taylor stared at the letter in her trembling hand, reading it again, allowing the words to wrestle their way into her brain. A chill dashed down her spine at the mention of her little girl. Rae was only five years old—an innocent in all this. Six months ago, Everleigh's world changed when her mother told her about the circumstances surrounding her conception. Deloris died a few days later on the first day of June.

Two weeks after her mother died, Everleigh received an offer from a small university in Charleston. She'd accepted the position as a professor of psychology, seizing the opportunity to build a new life for herself and Rae. A month after her mother's funeral, Everleigh left Savannah, Georgia, to escape her past and start fresh on Angel Island, located off the coast of South Carolina. She was no stranger to grief. Just one year prior to losing her mother, Everleigh's husband died, leaving her a widow at thirty. With both gone, the Hostess City of the South no longer felt like home.

Starting over in a new city brought hope, promise and no drama. She and her daughter were about to spend their first Christmas on the island. Everything had been going well, until today.

Her thirty-second birthday when she retrieved the letter from her mailbox.

She glanced down once more at the typewritten note in her hand, the words jumping out at her, the tone accusing and judgmental. It had been originally sent to her mother's home, then forwarded by the current occupants to her new address. According to Deloris, the only people who had known her father's identity were Deloris's parents, but clearly, there was someone else who knew the secret.

Who would want to hurt her and her child?

Her mind jumped to Wyle Gaines, a smooth talker who'd befriended Deloris at the hospital where they worked. He'd spent a lot of time with Deloris, even taking her to doctor appointments, cooking and staying with her whenever Everleigh had to work. Perhaps her mother had confided in him, which would explain how he knew the truth.

Everleigh had never cared for the man, but was unable to convince her mother that Wyle couldn't be trusted. When she'd put the house up for sale after her mother's death, he'd made an offer to purchase it at a substantially lower price than what it was worth.

When Everleigh refused him, Wyle became angry. He even claimed that Deloris had promised the house to him shortly after she got sick. Her mother had never mentioned this to Everleigh and she didn't believe a word of what

Wyle said. She ended up blocking him and threatened to call the police if he continued showing up at her door or her mother's home unannounced.

In the end, Everleigh rented out the house, choosing to keep the property. Was this his way of getting back at her for not letting him have her mother's house?

Everleigh bit back the overwhelming streak of panic she felt, refusing to allow her fear to spin out of control until she had a reason to be fearful.

She picked up her coat and purse, and headed out the door. Everleigh was going to the police precinct in Charleston. Declan Blanchet, a fellow professor at the university, was also a criminal investigator. She didn't know him well. Until now, they hadn't had any real interaction on campus other than general faculty meetings. She'd heard from some of the other staff that he was a decorated police detective, having been in law enforcement for fifteen years.

Everleigh turned up the heat in her car. She wasn't sure if the sudden chill was due to the wintry weather or the feeling of dread coursing through her veins.

She pulled into the parking lot of the Charleston police precinct. Everleigh sat in the car, debating whether she really wanted to see this through, to open this Pandora's box.

Five minutes later, she strode with purpose through the doors, walking up to a large desk that was separated from the public by a glass partition. While waiting for someone to assist her, Everleigh could hear sirens blaring from outside the building, competing against the anonymous voice coming through an intercom system. Behind her, the doors opened and closed in rapid succession.

"How may I help you?" a young woman in uniform asked. Her hair was braided down and pulled back into a bun.

"I'd like to speak with Detective Declan Blanchet. I work with him at the university."

"Your name?"

"Dr. Everleigh Taylor."

"Please have a seat over there, Dr. Taylor," the officer directed. "I'll let him know that you're here."

"Thank you," Everleigh said.

She sat down, her back straight. Her body was filled with tension.

Relax.

Everleigh went through a series of relaxation techniques while waiting to meet with Declan.

After all, the letter could turn out to be Wyle's idea of a cruel joke. He'd vowed to make her life miserable after she refused to sell him her mother's house. She reminded herself that until she knew the threat was real, there wasn't anything to worry about.

Her body however, revolted at the thought that he could be so cruel.

Forty-year-old Declan Blanchet's dark eyebrows rose to attention when he learned the woman requesting to speak with him was none other than Dr. Everleigh Taylor. She was the new professor in the psychology department. She was also extremely attractive and reserved, keeping mostly to herself whenever she was on campus. They'd said hello a few times, but hadn't interacted much otherwise.

He couldn't imagine why she'd come all the way to the precinct in Charleston to see him. He knew that she lived on Angel Island, two blocks from another colleague, Robin Rutledge, and the island had its own police department.

Declan walked past a couple of officers chatting over the sound of a microwave beeping in the break room.

"What's up, Blanchet?" one of them asked.

"Same thing, different day," he responded with a chuckle.

Declan peered through the locked door before walking out. Everleigh was dressed in a pair of gray designer jeans and a black turtleneck beneath a black wool coat. On her feet were a pair of leather loafers. He liked a woman who knew how to dress to accentuate her curves. Her hair was styled in the usual neat bun at her nape. Her skin was the color of smooth chocolate and free of makeup. Normally, she wore black-framed glasses, but not today.

He walked up and asked, "What can I do for you, Professor Taylor?"

"I think someone wants me and my daughter dead," Everleigh stated, getting straight to the point.

His jaw dropped. *I couldn't have heard her correctly.* "Excuse me?"

She handed him a piece of paper. "This letter was forwarded to me by the people renting my mother's house in Savannah. I have an idea of who might have sent it, but I'm not sure."

Declan's eyebrows shot up as he read the note, and he looked at Everleigh in disbelief. He led her to a deserted office, weaving through cubicles until they came to one with its door shut tight.

Inside, Everleigh spoke, almost too quietly for him to hear. "I found out six months ago that James Ray Powell is my father," she admitted.

He jolted. She didn't have to explain who the notorious serial killer was.

"My mother was one of his victims. She escaped with her life, but I was the result of the attack. She never reported it, and she told me that no one outside of her parents knew what happened. I think she may have told this guy. He spent quite a bit of time with her during her final days."

Declan swallowed his disbelief that someone as evil

as Powell could've fathered a woman like Everleigh. The man had raped and murdered as many as thirty women... maybe more. James Ray Powell began terrorizing Atlanta, Carrollton and a few other surrounding cities in Georgia in the mid-eighties. He was finally apprehended June 1990, six months before she was born.

"Who was the letter addressed to?" he inquired.

"My mother," she responded.

"It's possible that the letter is most likely referring to the two of you—mother and daughter."

"I had considered that," Everleigh said. "But this guy knows my mom is gone. Besides, she isn't related to Powell by blood—just me and Rae."

"We should consider all options. If it's not him, then I have to admit that I'm baffled," Declan said. "This is the first case I've heard about of a person seeking justice against a serial killer by going after the family members."

"So you don't think it's just some sick joke?" Everleigh asked.

"It's possible," he responded, though he had some reservations about the idea. "Have you told anyone about Powell?"

"No. It's not something I'd discuss—I'm disgusted by the very idea of that killer having fathered me. But this man...his name is Wyle Gaines. He worked at the hospital with my mom. He went out of his way to befriend her, although I never trusted him... Anyway, after she died, Wyle kept asking for different things—saying that she promised he could have them, including her house. He knew I'd never just sign it over to him, so he offered to purchase it for half of what it was worth. Wyle got very upset with me when I wouldn't sell to him."

"Did you ever feel threatened when he was around?" Declan asked.

"Not really," she responded. "Irritated mostly. But Wyle promised that he'd make life miserable for me."

"Do you think your mother told him about Powell?"

"It's entirely possible," Everleigh stated. "I'd like to think she wouldn't have told him anything, but my mother was under a lot of medication toward the end. She would say random things and she talked about Powell a lot in her final days."

He was surprised how calm Everleigh appeared to be about this situation, although he suspected that deep down, she was shaken.

"Detective Blanchet, I came to you to see if you can help with proving that this was sent by Wyle," she said. "It's crazy to think that there's someone out there who actually wants me dead because of a man I've never even met."

"Are you sure your mother never reported the attack?" Declan asked. "I believe there were only three victims known to have survived, but there is always the assumption that there could be more."

"According to what she told me, my mother left Atlanta that same night and never reported it. She said that she didn't know the identity of her attacker until after he'd been arrested."

"I'll investigate to determine if this is a real threat, or if this Wyle person is playing a sick prank on you," he said.

"I have no idea why he'd do something like this," she murmured bleakly. "It won't change my mind about my mother's house." Everleigh reached up and pushed away a dark, wavy tendril of hair that had escaped. "Thank you, Detective. I appreciate your time. I have to do whatever I can to protect my daughter."

"Please, call me Declan." He thought for a moment. "Is there anyone else who might hold a grudge against you? Have you ever been contacted by Powell himself?" The notorious killer was in prison for life, but he might try to contact those he believed to be family.

She shook her head. "I don't think there's any way he could know about us."

"Okay. I'll check out every avenue, including Gaines and Powell. We'll see what turns up."

"Only if you call me Everleigh," she responded with a smile. "As for Powell, I'd really like to leave him out of this. I don't want him to know about me, but especially about my daughter. I would never allow him into our lives."

"I'll be discreet. And, Everleigh, I want to assure you that nothing is going to happen to either of you under my watch," Declan said as he escorted her outside the busy precinct. "Does Wyle Gaines have your current address?"

"We weren't speaking at the point I'd decided to leave Savannah, so I didn't tell him anything. This letter was sent to the old address and forwarded to me here." Everleigh pulled the folds of her coat around herself to ward off the cold blast of wintry air. "Declan, thank you again. I wasn't sure if I should bother the police, in case it turned out to be nothing but someone ranting. But since we're colleagues, I thought it wouldn't hurt to ask."

He zipped up his black leather jacket. "My thoughts are that we don't need anyone else involved right now. I'll look into this personally."

"Please let me know as soon as you can if you find anything. Good or bad. I need to know everything."

"Okay. I'll let you know what I find."

Everleigh handed him a business card. "I wrote my home number on the back."

Declan watched as she walked briskly to her vehicle, unlocked the door and slid inside.

He hoped that the note she'd received would prove to be nothing, but he wasn't holding his breath.

TWO

It was still hard to digest the news of Powell being her father in addition to her grief. On top of that, Everleigh had to deal with Wyle's attempt to further manipulate her. Once Declan provided her with solid proof that it was him, she intended to petition the courts for a restraining order against Wyle. She was grateful Declan had agreed to look into the letter.

Everleigh wasn't so aloof that she didn't notice the outline of Declan's lean, muscular frame and long, powerful legs. His shaved head, warm mocha complexion, neatly trimmed mustache and beard… His face could have placed him on the list of the top ten most handsome men in the world.

In another life, Everleigh could appreciate a man as good-looking at Declan, but after losing her husband in the line of duty, she'd vowed to never give her heart to another *protector* type. She couldn't afford to put herself or Rae through another loss like that.

Everleigh made it back to the island in time to pick up her daughter from kindergarten.

"Hey, Mama," Rae greeted when she climbed into the back seat of the SUV. "Happy birthday! I made you a card."

Her heart warmed over her daughter's thoughtfulness. Rae was like her father—they preferred to make cards for special days like these. "Thank you, sweetie. Give it to me when we get home."

"Okay."

"How was your day?" Everleigh asked, looking into the rearview mirror. She waited patiently for Rae to secure her seat belt.

"Good," the little girl responded, her thick spiral curls covering her face.

Halfway down the street, she inquired, "Hey, where's your cap?"

"In my backpack," Rae answered. "I was about to get it out when you came."

Everleigh smiled to herself. Her daughter hated wearing caps and looked for any reason not to do so.

Ten minutes later, they were home. Once inside, Everleigh turned on the house alarm—it was something she normally didn't do until bedtime, but this letter had her spooked.

"Rae, do you remember what to do if we have uninvited visitors or I say Barbie's in trouble?"

She nodded. "I'm supposed to hide in my toy box—the one in the closet.

I use the phone in the toy box and call 911," Rae recited. "I tell the police we need help, then leave the phone on so they know where to find us."

"Now, remember that phone is only for emergencies," Everleigh reminded her. "I know how much you love playing games on my cell. I don't want you pulling it out for a quick game or two." She made a mental note to check the battery life. She kept it charged regularly.

"I know, Mama."

When she was growing up, Deloris had enrolled Everleigh in karate, and she'd eventually earned a black belt.

She understood now why her mother had been so concerned that she was able to defend herself.

"Mama, where are we going to eat?" Rae asked.

"I was thinking we'd just stay here."

"But we always go out for your birthday dinner."

"I thought we'd try something a little different," Everleigh said. "And we don't have to wait to eat birthday cupcakes because we'll already be home."

Rae beamed. "Yeah… I like that. But I still want to go out for my birthday dinner. I'll go get the menus out the kitchen drawer."

Grinning, she responded, taking a seat on the sofa to remove her shoes. "I know and that's fine." Rae's birthday wasn't until May, and Everleigh figured by then this mess with Wyle would be over. At least it was her fervent hope.

Anger washed over her in that moment. She didn't like having something like this hanging over her head. Her husband was gone and so was her mother. Everleigh's faith had gotten her through those heartbreaking losses, but how much more did she have to endure?

Rae interrupted her thoughts when she burst into the living room. "I hope we're ordering from Wings and More."

Everleigh's eyebrows rose in surprise. "You *want* hot wings?"

Nodding, Rae said, "You said it was your favorite place and it's your birthday."

She planted a kiss on her daughter's forehead. "You're such a sweetheart. I appreciate your thoughtfulness."

Everleigh placed their order, then stood up saying, "I'll make some veggies to go with our wings."

"Spinach," Rae suggested while skipping around. "I want spinach."

"Okay, sweetie. That's what we'll have. You know…you love vegetables but you don't like veggie pizza."

A grimace on her heart-shaped face, Rae responded, following her mother into the kitchen.

"Mama…some stuff don't go on pizza. Not good."

Everleigh smiled in amusement before opening the refrigerator for the container of spinach.

Just under an hour later, they were seated at the dining room table eating.

Everleigh checked her phone several times. She didn't want to miss a text or a call from Declan.

"I like the lemon-pepper ones best," Rae said.

"I thought you really liked the honey-barbecue wings."

"I do, but today I like this one best."

"You take after your grandmother," Everleigh said, a smile on her face. Deloris's mood often determined the flavor of her wings. She would order the sweet-chili or mango-habanero wings whenever she was happy and in a good mood. When she was upset about something, Deloris wanted naked wings. Whenever her mother felt daring, she would order the Nashville-hot or ghost-pepper wings.

"I wish Grandma and Daddy could be here with us, but I know they're in heaven having a party for your birthday."

Everleigh eyed her five-year-old daughter in awe. "I believe they are," she responded softly.

Rae finished off a wing, then asked, "Do you think God eats cupcakes?"

"Hmm… I'm not sure."

"I bet He does, Mama. Everything good and sweet comes from Him. That's what Daddy used to say."

Everleigh blinked back tears. "Your father was supersmart."

Rae nodded in agreement as she picked up another wing.

After they finished eating, Everleigh said, "Go wash your hands while I get the cupcakes."

"Don't forget that you have to blow out the candles first," Rae responded as she left the table. "And I have to sing 'Happy Birthday' to you, Mama."

She put cupcakes on each of their plates and stuck a candle on top of hers.

"I'm back," Rae announced, holding up her hands. "Clean."

"Good job, sweetie."

Everleigh blinked back tears as her little girl sang, "Happy birthday to you, happy birthday to you, happy birthday to yo-o-u-u... Happy birthday to you..."

She bent down to blow out the one candle.

"Did you make a wish?" Rae asked.

"I did."

Rae gave her the card she'd made. "And I have a present for you."

"You do?"

Rae grinned. "Yeah. I made it." She pulled a small box out of her pocket. "I wrapped it myself."

"You did a fabulous job."

Everleigh's eyes watered all over again when she saw the beaded bracelet her daughter made for her. "Oh, sweetie... I love it. And it's my favorite color. Purple."

"My friend and her sister helped me with it. Her sister makes them all the time."

She pulled Rae into her embrace. "You've made this birthday the best one *ever*. Thank you, my darling girl." Everleigh refused to allow anything to completely ruin this day for her.

When they readied for bed later that evening, she said, "I want you to sleep with me tonight."

"Yay!"

While Rae took her bath, Everleigh did another walk

through the house, making sure the windows and doors were all locked.

Everleigh checked the alarm again, since she'd turned it off briefly to accept their delivery order, then went back upstairs to her room. She checked the Taser in her nightstand drawer and the one stashed away inside a drawer in her bathroom.

She took a deep breath and forced her body to relax. She silently recited Psalm 91, then whispered, "Lord, I'm trusting You to keep us safe." Everleigh paused a moment, then added, "I hope You won't let me down again."

Declan sat in his office at the precinct, staring at the computer monitor the next morning. He was conducting a search on Wyle Gaines. The man had a couple of complaints for drunken behavior but no convictions. Another complaint came up. He was accused of taking advantage of an elderly woman. The family had filed a report that he'd swindled their elderly mother out of a large sum of money. However, when police had queried the woman, she'd admitted that she'd given the money to Wyle as a gift and refused to press charges.

Declan concluded that Wyle was most likely after the house and financial gain. He didn't doubt that the man would try to use fear tactics against Everleigh after she'd refused to give into his demands. But would he send a death threat?

He read the letter once more. The tone was chilling.

Somehow, Declan didn't believe it came from Wyle. He continued his investigation by calling the hospital where he worked.

"Savannah Memorial Medical Center…"

"I'd like to speak with Wyle Gaines."

"I'm sorry, but he doesn't work here anymore."

"When did he leave?" Declan asked.

"Five…six months ago. I'm not sure. Did you want to speak with someone else in the IT department?"

"No thanks. I'm a friend of his. We hadn't talked in a while. I'm in town for a few days and wanted to touch base."

"Oh, okay. Well, I'm sorry I can't be more help."

"It's fine," he said, then hung up.

"Where are you, Wyle Gaines?" he whispered.

For now, Declan decided to take the investigation in another direction.

He searched Powell's parents.

Ray Thomas Powell died a year after his son's arrest. The killer's seventy-year-old mother had died eleven months ago—Declan was relieved to see it was due to natural causes.

The next find, however, cooled his blood several degrees. Powell's oldest sister had been murdered in her home three months ago to the very day. Declan strongly considered the possibility that her death was simply a coincidence until his research led him to two other relatives in different cities also found dead in the past eight weeks—their deaths had been ruled homicides, but were unsolved. Both had arrest records, so again, it could just be a tragic happenstance. Besides, the methods of murder were different. The sister had been strangled. One of the relatives had been killed by gunshot, while the other had been bludgeoned to death. "No obvious connection between the murders," he whispered.

He checked to see whether any of the victims had received letters similar to Everleigh's. There wasn't any mention of it in the news. Declan hadn't expected there would be—it was not something he'd share with reporters if he was investigating the case.

Declan conducted a search through the National Integrated Ballistic Information Network to see if there were any matches to the bullets found at one of the crime scenes.

Next, he called and spoke with the investigators on all three murder cases. Declan decided to deliver what little information he'd found to Everleigh in person. He had been left with more questions than answers. He wished he had more definitive news for her.

Declan left his office shortly after one o'clock and drove to the university.

During the spring and summer months, the quad was covered in vibrant green grass crisscrossed by decorative pavers. Wooden benches were spaced along the pathway. He strolled past bike racks and plants in large pots toward a building with a decorative archway. However, the cordgrass was now a beautiful coppery brown.

Despite the biting December chill in the air, students sat outside alone or in groups; some walked to and from classes, oblivious to their surroundings. Banners hung over the pathway to the building next door.

Declan entered through the doors of the social-sciences building. He found Everleigh in her office.

"Good afternoon," she greeted when he knocked on her open door. "C'mon in."

"G' afternoon," he responded.

"Were you able to find anything out?" Everleigh asked when he sat down. "I know it's probably a long shot." She trained her eyes on him as if eager for information.

"I've found some concerning information. This may be more than the prank we'd hoped." Keeping his voice low so as not to be overheard, Declan said, "Powell's sister was murdered three months ago—she was strangled. Two other relatives in the last eight weeks. They all lived in different cities. The second victim—a cousin—was shot a couple of times. The third was involved in an altercation involving a woman a few hours before he was found bludgeoned to death. I spoke with the detectives on record for all three cases and was told that there weren't any letters found at the scenes."

Anxiety captured her body in a tight grip. "Do you think I was the only person who received one?" she asked.

"It just means they didn't find them. Still, there's a strong chance that those deaths could be random killings."

"And Wyle Gaines?"

"Your instincts about his motives toward your mother were on point. He manipulates and steals from women. There's no record of violence or threats. That being said, he could be behind this letter."

Everleigh rose to her feet and walked over to the window, then stood with her back to it.

"What do you think we should do?"

"I think it's best if we treat this threat as real."

She gave a stiff nod. "So what do I do now? I have classes and my daughter has school…" Her voice quavered, her body taut with dread.

"Have you seen anything out of the ordinary? Anything that may have stood out to you as strange at the time?"

"No, nothing," Everleigh responded. "And I'm always pretty observant of my surroundings. It's something my mother drilled into me."

"You can file an official report. We can assign an officer to watch your house. I'll arrange for campus security to walk you to and from your car."

Shaking her head, Everleigh said, "No, I'm not ready to do that. Declan, there's a chance that Wyle doesn't know where we are."

"I've had the letter dusted for prints," Declan said. "Hopefully, I'll hear something back soon."

Students began milling around outside her office.

"Why don't you come by my house this evening?" Everleigh suggested. "We can talk about this more in depth. If you don't have any plans, you're welcome to join us for dinner."

After agreeing to a time, Declan stood up. "I know you have to get ready for your class."

"I'll see you later."

She awarded him a smile. "Thanks for your help."

He smiled. "I'm happy to help."

As she prepared dinner, Everleigh recalled the many times she'd asked her mother about the identity of her father when she was growing up. All Deloris would ever tell her was that he'd died before she was born. She never pressed her mother for more information because it always seemed to upset her.

Two weeks before her death, Deloris had unburdened herself.

"Your father is James Ray Powell," she had revealed.

Everleigh swallowed hard, then asked in a disbelieving voice, "You're talking about the serial killer?"

Her mother gave a faint nod, which seemed to sap her strength.

Everleigh felt her knees go weak, like she was going to collapse. She practically fell into the chair by her mother's hospital bed.

"Did you love him?" she asked with a shaky voice.

"Love him? No… He raped me, Evvie… He would've killed me…" Her mother's voice warbled with emotion, the words taking most of her strength. "That night, all I could do was ask the Good Lord for help. I fought him with everything in me but he overpowered me. When it was over, I got to the gun my daddy gave me and started shooting… I don't know if I hit him. He ran off. Never knew his identity until I saw his picture on television after he was arrested sometime later. God protected me from a worse fate."

Deloris rested a moment before continuing.

"It's not something I ever wanted to talk about or even tell you…" Her eyes watered.

"Evvie, I just couldn't take this to the grave. Had to clear my conscience. I want you to know that it doesn't matter who fathered you. I loved you from the moment I found out I was pregnant. When they placed you in my arms, my heart leaped with joy."

Then, Deloris had drifted off to sleep, the medication finally melting away her pain.

Everleigh didn't doubt her mother's love, and she hated that Deloris had been weighed down with this secret for so long. Her mother never intended to tell her about Powell, but for some reason, she'd changed her mind at the end.

Humming softly to soothe herself, Everleigh checked on the chicken breasts in the air fryer. It wouldn't be long before they were ready. She glanced at the clock on the wall. Declan was due to arrive within the next fifteen minutes.

"Mama, who's coming to eat with us?" Rae asked when she strolled into the kitchen. "You put three placemats on the table."

"A friend from the university. His name is Professor Blanchet. He and I have some business to discuss afterward, so I need you to go on and get your bath out of the way. Pick out what you want to wear to school tomorrow."

"Mama, I wanna sleep in your room again."

"That's fine, sweetie," Everleigh said. The truth of it was that she would sleep better with her daughter right beside her.

She checked on Rae a few times as she prepared din-

ner and did a cursory sweep of her house. There wasn't a
speck of dust to be seen; her home looked picture-perfect.
She returned to the kitchen and wiped down the counter
for the second time. Or was it the third? Cleaning often
aided in calming her nerves.

This wasn't a social visit, Everleigh reminded herself.
I'm not looking to impress him.

The doorbell sounded a couple of minutes after 7:00 p.m.

She walked briskly to the well-lit foyer, then peered
through the peephole before opening the front door.

"Welcome to my home," Everleigh said, stepping aside
to let Declan enter.

Her daughter joined them in the foyer, sparking a hint
of amusement in his expression.

"This is Rae."

Declan smiled. "It's very nice to meet you. I'm—"

"*Perfessor* Blanchet," the little girl said, finishing for
him. "You work with my mama."

"Beautiful and brilliant," he said.

"Yes," Rae responded with a grin.

Everleigh gestured for him to follow her into the living
room. A charcuterie tray and plates were sitting on the coffee table. She placed some meat, cheese and a couple of
crackers on a plate for Rae, who then sat quietly beside her.

Everleigh and Declan made small talk while nibbling
on the appetizers. She forced her body to relax. It had been
a while since she'd entertained such a handsome man. He
didn't come off as flirty. Just professional.

He had changed into a pair of jeans and a black sweatshirt with the university logo emblazoned in red. She'd
been given one just like it, only hers was in a vivid shade
of red with the logo in black.

She stood up and said, "I need to check on dinner. I'll
be back shortly."

Everleigh zipped into the kitchen, retrieved the pan of yeast rolls from the oven and placed it on a warming rack. She swept crumbs from the counter into her hand to transport them to the sink.

Ten minutes later, they gathered around the dining room table.

Rae volunteered to bless the food.

"Amen. Great job," Everleigh said when she finished.

Her daughter kept the conversation lively while they ate.

"Do you like being a *perfessor*?"

"I do," Declan responded. "I enjoy teaching."

"My teacher is mean," Rae announced.

Everleigh chuckled. "No, she's not. Miss Davis is just a bit strict."

Shrugging, her daughter responded, "She don't know how to have fun. I miss my old teacher, Miss Pitts. She was funny and she liked to sing."

They chatted for a bit about Rae's school and her favorite songs. Then, taking a decisive bite, Declan said, "Dinner is delicious."

"Mama's a real good cook," Rae stated. "You have to eat her oatmeal-raisin cookies and her choc'late peanut-butter brownies. They're so-o-o good."

He grinned. "I'll have to remember that."

Everleigh kept her gaze on her plate, not wanting to become absorbed in Declan's attractive features. However, she took pride in her cooking skills and was glad he seemed to be enjoying his food.

When they finished eating, Everleigh and Declan carried the plates into the kitchen. She quickly rinsed them, then placed them into the dishwasher.

After sending her daughter upstairs, she said, "I never mentioned that you were also a police detective. I didn't want to confuse Rae."

"I figured as much," he responded while leaning against the island countertop. "Oh, there weren't any matches on the prints."

"Because that would be too easy," Everleigh muttered almost to herself.

They walked the short distance to the living room and sat down to finish their conversation.

"You may be right about the individual not knowing where you are. Right now, it seems you're safe."

"I hope it stays that way."

"Tell me everything you know about your mother's encounter with Powell," Declan said.

"I don't know very much," Everleigh responded. "He attacked her and if she hadn't been able to get to the gun she kept in her nightstand, Powell most likely would've killed her. Because she never pressed charges, the police didn't know that she was another victim who'd survived his death sentence." She looked Declan in the eye. "I really don't want this getting out to anyone. I especially don't want Powell learning that he has a daughter and grand-daughter out here."

"I'll do what I can. But if we have to get the police more officially involved…the truth is going to come out, especially if arrests are made."

"I really don't want to think about that right now." Everleigh was mostly concerned about what this would do to her daughter. Families of violent criminals were often ill-prepared to deal with the complex set of emotions that come with being related to a murderer; and then there were accusations and threats by those seeking justice. People that would send letters like the one she received.

"I checked on Wyle Gaines. He left his job at around the same time you left Savannah."

A wave of anxiety washed over Everleigh. "Do you know where he is?"

"I don't, sorry."

"So what are you thinking, Declan?"

"At first, I liked Wyle for this. I'm not as sure now. I don't believe he had anything to do with the deaths of Powell's relatives, and that bothers me."

"Then you don't think they were random?" Everleigh asked.

"I don't," Declan said. "My gut is telling me there's something bigger at play here."

"So while it's possible that he could've sent the letter to me as an isolated incident, there actually *is* someone out there killing Powell's relatives?"

He nodded. "I believe there's a vigilante on the loose."

"It must be one of Powell's surviving victims," Everleigh replied. "Or a family member of a victim. Wyle is manipulative, a thief and a liar, but he isn't a killer. I still think he's capable of sending a threatening letter, however."

"I'm going to look into the family members of the victims."

She smoothed a hand over her hair. "Declan, I know we don't know each other well, but I really appreciate you helping me out like this. I didn't know who to ask, but I've heard nothing but good things about you around the campus. I really believe that you're the right person for this."

"I'm honored you feel comfortable enough to trust me with this."

"So what happens next?"

"I'll keep looking," Declan replied. "And if something's there, I will find it."

"I need to check on my daughter. I'll be right back."

He smiled and nodded.

Upstairs, she found Rae in bed playing on her tablet. "You're supposed to be sleeping," Everleigh said.

Rae looked up. "Can I play for a little longer please?"

"Okay. But when I come back up—it's lights out."

Rae sighed. "Okay Mama…"

Everleigh kissed her daughter on the forehead before returning downstairs.

"That little girl does not like going to bed before ten o'clock."

"I was just like that when I was a kid," Declan responded.

Thinking back to the reason for his being there, Everleigh said, "This probably sounds terrible but I was really hoping you'd find Wyle's prints on that letter. It's not that I want to… I'm not sure what I'm trying to say."

"You would rather it be him because the alternative is much worse."

"Yes. That's it exactly."

"Either way, you don't have to face this alone," Declan assured her.

She was comforted by his words, and their conversation turned to something more pleasant. The university. They talked about their experiences teaching, their students and classes. When Everleigh looked up at the clock, she was surprised to see the time ticking closer to eleven. She felt her cheeks grow hot with embarrassment for having monopolized his time for so long. "I didn't realize it was so late already."

He stood, too. "Yeah, I'd better get going. I know it was for a grim reason, but I enjoyed tonight. Thank you for a wonderful evening, Everleigh."

"I want you to know that you're my first dinner guest."

Declan broke into a grin. "Wow. You honor me once again."

Everleigh walked him to the door.

"Go through and make sure the windows and doors are locked securely," he said.

"I will," she responded. "That's my nightly routine. I'm also setting my alarm."

After Declan left, Everleigh made sure everything was secured before arming her security system.

Upstairs, she found Rae in the middle of her king-size bed fast asleep. Everleigh stood there watching her just like she had when she was a baby. Both then and now, her daughter's safety was her primary concern.

Everleigh took a quick shower, leaving the bathroom door wide open, then joined her daughter in bed.

She closed her eyes and tried to relax. A tremor exploded through Everleigh as thoughts about Declan flooded her mind. She was grateful that she didn't have to navigate this situation alone. Just before the winter break at the university, he'd been nothing more to her than a member of the faculty. But now, she was beginning to consider him a friend, a confidant.

Everleigh hoped Declan would be able to figure out everything without having to put on an official police-detective hat.

THREE

Declan felt himself smile as he drove home from Everleigh's. He'd learned a lot about Dr. Taylor just from the decor. Large cranberry-hued curtain-framed windows welcomed in natural light. He'd read somewhere that individuals exposed to natural light on a daily basis experienced fewer headaches, and less eye strain and blurred vision. Her beige sofa was plush and comfortable with several throw pillows in neutral colors. An overstuffed matching chair with a rich cranberry-red throw folded over the arm sat near the cream-colored stone fireplace. He knew that neutral colors had a calming effect on a person. It was obvious that Everleigh relished a life that wasn't hectic or crowded. She used her environment to help usher in a sense of peace all around her.

On the drive back to Charleston, Declan recalled how much he'd really enjoyed spending time with the beautiful professor and her daughter. He found Rae delightful. But the evening also reminded him of what was missing in his life. He was forty years old. Declan wanted to start a family while he was still physically able to enjoy spending time with them.

It was clear that Everleigh and Rae lived alone. He'd heard that Everleigh was a widow, and he felt a touch of sadness when he thought of sweet little Rae growing up without her father. Declan vowed to protect them both to the best of his ability. However, he feared that meant he'd eventually have to make the investigation an official one. The only reason he hadn't thus far was because there was no obvious connection in the deaths to prove serial killings. Sure, the anchor point was that the victims were related to Powell, but there weren't any other letters like the one Everleigh received. Declan knew she didn't want people knowing about her relationship to Powell, and as much as he wanted to respect this decision, his priority was their safety.

An image of Everleigh formed in his mind. She had a really beautiful smile. It was funny that he'd never noticed it before, but then they hadn't had much interaction in the past. Declan especially enjoyed watching her with Rae. She seemed to be a very loving mother and he could see that they were close.

Dinner with them had offered him a preview of what life might look like if he got married. Declan had never been opposed to the idea—he just hadn't found the right woman. At one point, he'd thought he met her, but no... He'd never been more wrong. He'd ended up with a broken heart and had taken the past couple of years away from dating to heal.

Declan cautioned himself not to think about Everleigh in this manner. She was only interested in his help.

Not his heart.

Still, he found himself attracted to her courage and strength. Everleigh wasn't a wilting flower, shrinking in fear. Instead, she wanted to face this threat head-on. Declan was still smiling as she continued to dominate his thoughts. Her warm and friendly manner was contagious.

Declan could only describe the feeling he got when they

were together earlier as *coming home*. He felt like a different person. He forced her out of his mind because he wasn't looking to get involved with her. He was committed to keeping Everleigh and her daughter safe.

The next morning, Everleigh dropped Rae at kindergarten, then headed back home since her first class wasn't until ten. Since she had some time on her hands, Everleigh searched her brain for a way to show gratitude for Declan's help.

She recalled his mentioning at a faculty brunch how much he loved the combination of chocolate and peanut butter. Rae had mentioned it as well when he had dinner with them. She decided that her chocolate peanut-butter brownies would be the perfect gift.

Humming softly, she walked into her kitchen and grabbed the ingredients, then set them on the island counter, where a rack of copper pots and pans dangled overhead.

Everleigh mixed ingredients in a purple ceramic bowl with a large wooden spoon. She found herself glancing around, eyeing the items she could use as weapons if necessary. Everleigh was determined that fear would not take control of her life. It was normal to feel afraid in the presence of real danger. But it would not overtake her.

Steam wafted from the coffee maker behind her.

Everleigh stopped long enough to pour her second cup of coffee of the morning. She leaned back against the counter, savoring the French-vanilla flavor and admiring the new dishware arranged neatly on the open shelves. A clear stand held knives and shears with purple-and-chrome handles.

Bananas, apples and oranges intermingled with miniature boxes of raisins looked picture-perfect in the chrome wire-framed basket in the center of the island. A calendar marked up and color-coded with appointments, events, school holidays and special reminders popped up on the touch screen of her refrigerator.

If only I could check that letter off my list as solved. She'd like nothing better than to be on the other side of this situation, but until she was, Everleigh vowed to keep life normal for herself and Rae. She refused to be a victim.

She poured the batter into a baking dish and placed it in the oven. Everleigh set the timer, then rushed up the stairs to shower and dress for work.

The brownies were done shortly after she came back down, dressed in a black pencil skirt and matching jacket, a lavender silk blouse and a pair of black boots. She left the house twenty-five minutes later, heading for the university.

At the university, Everleigh waved at another faculty member on her way from the parking lot to her office. She stopped at the nameplate fastened to the wall with her name engraved on it. She unlocked the door, then opened it and entered.

A desk and rolling leather chair greeted her warmly. Everleigh loved teaching. She loved her job. In one corner of her office sat a box containing extra office supplies. The only things on her desk were a printer, calculator, phone and a couple photographs of Rae. Her laptop was in her tote—she carried it home with her every day.

Everleigh glanced out the window, watching students as they gathered in small groups to chat or made their way across campus to their next class.

A chill snaked down her spine when she spied a tall man in black hoodie and sweatpants beneath a nearby tree. He seemed to be watching the building. From a distance, he looked like Wyle.

Everleigh turned and strode toward the door. She rushed outside, only to find the man was gone.

Her eyes traveled the area, searching. She saw several students dressed in dark hoodies. Her anxiety high, Everleigh forced herself to relax. She glanced around a second time.

No sign of Wyle.

She went back to her office.

Everleigh removed the container of brownies from her tote, then checked her watch. Declan's next class was in forty-five minutes. She wanted to catch him before it started.

Leaving her coat draped over the back of her chair, she started toward his office.

She almost turned around, worried he might misread her intentions. But, no, she was being ridiculous.

He's a smart man. Declan will know that this is just a token of my appreciation. He's not expecting anything more from me.

She paused outside of his office and took a deep, cleansing breath.

Declan was just finishing up with office hours. He'd walked one student through an extra credit assignment to help her make up for an exam she'd failed and shared tips on criminology careers with another. This student was a little older than the undergrads he'd met with so far, maybe in his thirties.

Of average height and build, he looked as if he took great care of his body. Athletic and possibly military judging from his cross-cropped haircut and posture.

"I just wanted to introduce myself, sir," the man said. He pushed back the hood of his thick gray sweatshirt. "I'm Aaron Edwards. I'll be starting here in January and I'm planning to take your class next semester. I just got out of the military a few months ago—military police."

"Thank you for your service to this country, Aaron. It's

nice to meet you. You sound like a man who knows exactly what he wants."

"I've always wanted to be a criminologist."

"I look forward to having you in class," Declan responded.

He smiled. "Same here, Professor."

He walked the younger man to the door, intending to head out to teach his next class.

Everleigh was in the doorway. He broke into a grin.

She smiled at Aaron as he exited, then turned a bigger smile on him.

"I wanted to show my appreciation for your help, so I baked you some brownies." She held out the container to him.

"Chocolate and peanut butter?" Declan asked, sniffing.

"Yes," she responded. "I remembered you mentioning that you love chocolate and peanut butter during the brunch last month. Then when Rae mentioned my cookies the other night at dinner, you seemed to light up."

"That's because chocolate peanut butter anything are my favorites. Thank you," Declan said, smiling. "I'm not sure they're going to make it by the time I leave for the precinct after this class."

Everleigh chuckled. "As long as you enjoy them."

"How are you doing?" Declan asked. "Really?"

"It depends on the hour," she replied with a slight shrug. "For the most part, I find myself constantly looking over my shoulder. More than usual. Like, I was looking out my office window when I saw this guy in a black hoodie and sweatpants. Somehow, I thought it was Wyle. I went out to confront him and the guy was gone."

"You're going to find students in dark hoodies all over the campus."

"I know," Everleigh responded. "The only reason he stood out was because he seemed to be watching the building."

"Are you sure it was Wyle?" He made a mental note to check to see if Wyle was still in Savannah. As long as he hadn't left town, Declan could rule him out as a suspect.

"I wish I could say that I am, but no. I'm not sure."

"I am going to do everything in my power to keep you and Rae safe."

Everleigh eyed him. "Thank you, Declan. I've been wondering if Wyle is planning to blackmail me with the information he has."

"I've been thinking about that myself and I checked on something. Powell has been incarcerated in a maximum-security prison outside of Reidsville, Georgia, for almost thirty-one years. He hasn't had any visitors in the past year. I don't think he and Wyle could have been in touch."

"I hope you're not thinking of going down there to talk to him," she uttered. "I don't want him knowing anything about me or my daughter, Declan."

"I understand, but you should be prepared in case the truth comes out."

Everleigh gave a slight wave of her hand in dismissal. "I don't want to think about that right now." She folded her arms across her chest.

He nodded. "Gaines might have conducted a search on real estate. He could have found you that way. He might also have found you on the university's department page."

She sighed. "This is my first teaching job," Everleigh stated. "I worked as a psychologist for a counseling center in Savannah. I've done that since graduating from college. The minute I have an online presence, he found me. That's one of the reasons why I'm not a fan of social media."

"It certainly works in your favor," Declan stated.

"Hopefully, all this might turn out to be nothing," she said. "That's my prayer."

"Mine, too. Thank you for these brownies."

Everleigh glanced up at the clock on the wall. "I guess I'd better get out of here. I need to get to my class before my students or I'll never hear the end of it." She slipped the tote on her shoulder. "Please let me know if you learn anything more."

"Will do," Declan agreed.

He sat the brownies down on his desk, then left his office. As much as he wanted to sample one, Declan decided to exercise self-control and wait.

When class ended, so did his self-control. Declan opened the Tupperware container and bit into a brownie. He closed his eyes, his tastebuds exploding with delight as he chewed. He quickly devoured a second one as he walked in quick strides toward the faculty parking lot. His entrance into the police precinct fifteen minutes later was met with friendly smiles and nods as he made his way to his office. He waved in passing to a sergeant as he strolled by his open door.

He'd come in an hour earlier to get a head start on his day. Declan wanted to make some calls regarding Powell. He needed to find out as much information about his victims and their families—all of them, including the ones who survived.

What stumped Declan most was how the connection to Everleigh was made. Especially since no one outside of her parents knew that Powell was her father. Her mother must have confided in Wyle. It was the only theory that made sense.

FOUR

Knowing that Declan was looking into the letter had placed Everleigh somewhat at ease. In the short amount of time that she's spent with him, she could tell he was definitely a "protector" type. Her late husband had been, too, which led to him becoming a firefighter—a job that cost him his life.

Declan was handsome—she'd always been attracted to men with bald heads, neatly trimmed beards and mustaches. She didn't *want* to like him in that manner, though. The last thing on Everleigh's mind was a relationship. Her focus was on keeping Rae safe while trying to find out who wanted to harm them, and then making sure they were comfortable in their new lives here. Because even under different circumstances, she wasn't interested in a relationship with someone with a high-risk job.

Everleigh ushered the last student in her class to the door, then made her way back to her office. She slumped down into her office chair and dug into the insulated lunch bag she'd stashed under her desk that morning. Sighing softly, she put up her feet on the cushioned stool below her the desk as she ate her sandwich.

It had been a long morning. She'd finally convinced herself that she'd dreamed up the vision of Wyle on campus.

From there, she'd gone from talking a student into believing that she could pass the upcoming final if she put more time in studying and taking good notes, to advising another that he needed to rewrite his final paper before the due date. Between classes and appointments, Everleigh managed to offer advice to a coworker who wanted to think that the assistant football coach half her age was sincere in his pursuits. She'd advised the woman to take things slow.

Excitement did not bubble in Everleigh's chest as she popped the lid off the container of raw carrots. She'd rather have had a large bag of potato chips to eat with the accompanying ranch dip, but she was trying to change her eating habits. Her recent birthday had her thinking seriously about the importance of a healthy lifestyle. Everleigh was satisfied with her weight—she had a high metabolism, which kept her looking trim, but there were some creases, wrinkles and folds that hadn't been there in her younger years.

She bit into the carrot stick, chewing thoughtfully as she took a moment to distance herself from the contents of the letter she'd received, to form an unbiased analysis.

Wyle Gaines wasn't the person who'd sent the letter. The sender was angry; the individual couldn't get to Powell because he was in a maximum-security facility, so they'd decided to take another route. Everleigh had recently lectured on displaced anger, which happened when someone directed their hostility away from its cause toward something or someone else.

She had explained to her students that the source of most displaced anger stemmed from adverse childhood events, which caused a disruption in a person's healthy emotional development and regulation. The sender could have experienced abuse or bullying. In some scenarios they might even have been a witness or victim of extreme violence.

As a therapist, Everleigh had dealt with clients experiencing displaced anger. They came to see her to learn how to manage their frustrations, to disengage from difficult situations. She knew how to handle a situation like that, but none of her clients were ever violent or threatening.

That wasn't to say she didn't know how to deal with scarier situations. Deloris had enrolled Everleigh in self-defense classes when she was younger. Deloris had insisted on her staying in karate all through her teen years. With her black belt, she could handle herself. She also had weapons, if need be. Everleigh possessed two bats and she was adept with a knife and Taser. She kept several Tasers hidden around her home for protection. She also had her mother's gun, but Everleigh wasn't a fan of firearms. Deloris's gun was packed away with some of her things in a local storage facility. She wasn't quite ready to get rid of her mother's stuff.

Everleigh glanced at the clock on her office wall, then dropped her feet to the floor. She had to meet with two more students and teach another class before she could leave campus for the day.

While her time was still her own, Everleigh left her office to visit the bookstore. There were a couple of orders waiting for pickup.

On the way back to the social-sciences building, Everleigh pulled out her ringing cell phone. Without looking at the screen, she said, "Professor Taylor speaking..."

She heard heavy breathing on the other end.

"Wyle, this isn't funny."

Everleigh hung up. The number wasn't local, and the area code wasn't a Georgia one, but she was pretty sure it had to be him.

Frustrated, she dropped her purchases in her office before walking briskly to the classroom. Everleigh took several calming breaths while waiting for students to arrive.

She liked being punctual, so once everyone was seated, Everleigh dove right in. "Last week we discussed the seven approaches to the study of abnormal psychology—"

A shot rang out. Glass shattered and someone screamed. Everleigh shouted to her students, "Get down!"

They dropped to the ground, taking cover where they could. Anxiety fluttered in her chest and her heart jolted. "Remember the active-shooter protocol," she said. "Stay down and move toward the exit doors."

She was about to step out of her room when the building's security guard arrived, his face set with determination as he motioned for her to stay down and away from the door. Drawing his gun, he cautiously eased the double doors of her lecture room open.

The shooter fired a second shot.

"Someone is shooting into my class," Everleigh said.

The guard signaled for her and the students to stay low and get out. "Keep the students inside the building."

She did as instructed.

The exits had all been locked so no one could enter without a key.

Everleigh urged the students to find a safe place and stay there. Another faculty member directed them to the auditorium.

A third shot rang out…

Everleigh quickly ushered the frightened students to the auditorium, her voice trembling as another gunshot sounded.

Amidst the chaos, she heard a pounding on a door at the entrance. She saw a student with a cast on his foot outside, stark fear etched over his face. Adrenaline coursed through

Everleigh's veins as she rushed forward to assist him into the building. She quickly slammed the door closed, locking it once more.

She waited for the ringing in her ears to stop, the light-headedness to pass and the knot in her stomach to ease. She stood trembling against the wall.

"Was anyone hurt?" someone in the vicinity asked.

"That last bullet hit one of the huge pots in the front," the young man wearing the cast responded shakily.

Thirty minutes passed without gunfire.

Everleigh ventured outside with a member of security, her gaze falling on the shattered remains of a terra-cotta pot that had been knocked off its perch by a bullet. Jagged shards of clay littered the sidewalk, while mangled leaves from the plant lay scattered around it like casualties of war. She wanted to close her eyes and pretend it was all a bad dream, but she couldn't.

Someone had just tried to kill her.

Where is Rae?

She had to get to her daughter. The college had activated their active-shooter safety protocols, but she had to find out if her daughter was safe. Security urged everyone to stay away from the doors and windows, so she crept carefully back to her office and called the school.

"Hey, this is Everleigh Taylor. I just wanted to check on Rae. Is she okay?"

"Oh, she's fine. Her class just came inside for snacks."

"That's great. I'll be there within the hour. I'm picking her up early today." Her appointments and class were canceled for the rest of the afternoon.

Everleigh hung up, then walked over to the campus police officer waiting to speak with her. She wanted to get this over with, so she could get to Rae. It wouldn't take long because there wasn't much she could tell them.

She wanted desperately to believe this was some random shooting, but Everleigh knew better. This, coupled with the sighting of Wyle on campus... The two had to be connected. Maybe he was willing to kill for her mother's house after all.

Declan received an alert about the shooting and was headed back to the campus. A black truck sped past him toward the university exit, but he wasn't able to catch a real glimpse at the Maryland license plate.

Students were running, panic and fear written all over their faces. Campus security was all over the grounds.

Declan released a sigh of relief when he found Everleigh inside the building talking to a couple of campus police officers. He quickened his steps to join them.

"Are you okay?" he asked.

"I'm a bit shaken, but I'm fine."

"Was anyone hurt?"

"No, thank goodness," she responded. "Class had just started when two bullets came through the window. The third was fired at the front of the building. Officer Mack was just saying that it was most likely a random shooting." Her expression told him that she believed otherwise, but didn't want to say too much around the campus security officer.

When the officer walked away, Declan pulled her off to the side where they couldn't be overheard. "I think it's time we make this investigation official. Especially if someone just fired shots at you."

Swallowing hard, she gave a slight nod. "I know. I'm thinking Wyle is behind all this. I wasn't sure earlier if I'd really seen him, but now I'm convinced it was him. Probably wanting to scare me."

"Why don't I drive you home?" Declan suggested. "You

can leave your car here." Everleigh was trying to display a calm he knew she didn't currently possess. She was playing with her wedding rings and her eyes darted from person to person.

"You don't have to do that," she said. "I have to pick up Rae from school. I can go to the precinct now if it's not going to take too long to file a report."

"It won't. I'll get you in and out as quickly as I can."

She gave him a tiny smile. "Let me check to see if I can leave."

Everleigh went to speak with the campus police before walking with Declan to the faculty parking area.

He followed her to the precinct and parked beside her.

"What if we're wrong about this?" she said as they approached the entrance. "Maybe the campus police were right. It could've been someone just firing a random shot. I'd rather not waste time filing a report."

"I only have to look in your eyes to know that you don't really believe what you just said. Everleigh, you're scared."

"I… You're right. I'm scared, Declan. But I'm not going to let anyone have that kind of power over me. I'm also angry."

"Would you consider teaching virtually? We can also arrange for police protection around the clock for the next forty-eight hours and reevaluate the threat after that."

"I guess I don't have a choice," she responded. "I'd like to keep Rae in school, though. If I have to take her out— I can tell you that she's not going to be happy about this. My daughter's a social butterfly."

Declan smiled to reassure her. "I'm hopeful that it won't be for too long, but I think it's best she stay home with you."

"Okay. And I'd like to help," Everleigh stated. "I can't just sit and do nothing. I intend to find out everything I can about Powell and his victims—at least the ones we know about. I can't help but wonder if there are others who survived his attack but didn't report it."

"No other women came forward during his trial," Declan responded. "I checked."

Everleigh paced in the waiting area while he went to speak with one of his colleagues. Her eyes traveled to the American flag, Rotary Club plaques and framed map of Charleston County hanging behind the huge desk with a glass partition. Two officers, one male and the other female, were sitting at the desk and checking in visitors.

Public bathrooms and water fountains were situated to Everleigh's left. On her right, a door with a keypad and electronic lock led deeper into the precinct. It was the door Declan had disappeared behind.

Phones rang, the officers talked in quiet tones, keyboards clicked and the shuffling of paper echoed in the sparsely decorated waiting room. Her nostrils caught a whiff of sweat and body odor from a homeless man as he walked past her.

Everleigh glanced up at the clock on the wall, wishing Declan would suddenly reappear. Every time the electronic door clicked and opened; her hopes were dashed when it wasn't him.

Hip-hop music seeped out of the earbuds of a woman who was seated in front of her. Every now and then, Everleigh heard a police radio shrieking interlaced with a baby crying. A couple behind her were embroiled in a heated argument she hoped wouldn't soon get out of hand.

She'd begun to experience a jittery sensation and the hair at her nape stood at attention. Someone was watching her.

Everleigh's gaze slowly traveled her surroundings. Her

body stiffened when she found the homeless man staring in her direction. He gave her a toothless grin.

She awarded him a small smile before looking away. She didn't want to provoke him if he was violent, or insult him if he was harmless.

As soon as Declan walked out, Everleigh jumped up and met him halfway. "I'm so glad to see you," she whispered. "That homeless man has been staring at me since he sat down."

"Did he say anything to you?"

"No, he just sat there looking. If I looked in his direction, he'd grin."

"That's Ralph. He's been here a few times," Declan said. "His things are always stolen whenever he stays at the mission. He comes to file a report."

"So he's more of a precinct regular," Everleigh responded. "Does he have any family?"

"He's in here at least once every other week. As for family, I don't think so. After his wife died, he just kind of lost himself."

"That's so sad," she murmured.

Keeping his voice low, Declan said, "I spoke to my supervisor, who contacted the chief on the island. There will be an officer parked outside your house while you're in what's considered a high-threat situation." He led her to a conference room. "I'll work on your report in here. I'll also email a copy to the precinct on the island."

"I really can't believe this is my life right now," Everleigh stated when Declan finished with the report. "My mom didn't like me working at the counseling center. She thought it was dangerous."

He got up, retrieved two bottles of water and handed one to her. "Is that why you decided to change careers?"

"Not at all," she answered. "After my mom died, I just felt

like I needed to do a complete reset with my life. I wanted to start over fresh."

"I get that. I felt the same way but for different reasons. I wanted to find a way to help and educate people. I enjoyed mentoring young men, so teaching seemed the next step for me."

Declan filled out the report as they talked. When they were done, she asked, "Do you like being a criminal investigator?"

"I do. I love it," Declan replied. "I studied criminology because I love science, psychology and law—I'm able to combine all of them in my job.

I've always been interested in the causes of crime and ways to prevent and control it—that's why I majored in criminology, and I also have a degree in criminal psychology."

"Where the focus is on studying the thoughts, feelings and behaviors of criminals," Everleigh responded. "There was a time when I was interested in forensic psychology, but as you can imagine, my mother was totally against it. Now that I know what happened to her, I can understand her reaction. I always thought she was being too overprotective... bordering on being a helicopter mom." She released a sigh. "I should've known it ran deeper than that. She was dealing with trauma."

"I hope you're not carrying any guilt over this. Because it's not your fault, Everleigh."

Looking up at him, she replied, "Maybe I could've helped her."

"She didn't want you to know."

Declan escorted Everleigh outside to her vehicle. "I'm gonna head over to the island to the station. I want to meet with the officers personally."

"Thank you for everything."

Everleigh left the parking lot. She noticed a black SUV that pulled behind her, and admired the glossy richness of the color.

She picked up Rae twelve minutes later from school.

"Mama, can I play on your iPad?"

"Hello to you, too."

"Hey, Mama," Rae responded, a sheepish grin on her face. "Sorry."

"That's better," she said. "It's in my tote back there."

It wasn't until Everleigh took the exit toward the freeway that she spotted the same SUV behind her.

Are they following me?

She glanced into the rearview mirror, making sure Rae was secured in her seat. She then gave the command. "Call Declan."

When he answered, she asked, "Where are you?"

"I'm at the Angel Island precinct. Have you made it home yet?"

"There was a black SUV behind me when I left the precinct. It's still behind me," Everleigh said, keeping any emotion out of her voice. She didn't want to scare her daughter.

The SUV was now directly behind her.

She increased her speed.

"I'm about to cross the bridge."

"Come to the precinct," Declan instructed. "If they're still behind you, I can take it from there."

"Okay." She eyed Rae in the rearview mirror.

The little girl's attention was glued to her iPad game.

"I'm about to cross the bridge. I'll see you soon."

The SUV inched closer—too close for comfort.

Everleigh increased her speed, hoping to put some distance between herself and the SUV. She was relieved when another vehicle separated them. She sped up and went around a bus.

She took the exit to the precinct and didn't bother slowing down. The best thing that could happen in this moment was running into the police.

The SUV was back behind her.

Everleigh scanned the parking lot of the precinct when she arrived and quickly spotted Declan standing beside his car.

She hastily parked in the space next to him and cast a furtive glance back, watching as the suspicious vehicle slowly drove past the entrance.

Declan got into his car, then called her cell.

All he said when she answered, "I'm following you home."

Everleigh took a deep breath and responded with a trembling wave of relief, "Glad to hear it."

"Mama, what are we doing here?" Rae asked, looking around. "We're at a police station."

"No reason. It's the wrong address," she responded. "We're heading home now."

"Good. I'm hungry."

Everleigh forced a smile at her daughter in the rearview mirror. "We'll be home soon."

As she steered them home, she noted that Declan was a car behind them, but she viewed every dark SUV as suspect. She conjured the image of the vehicle that had followed her. She was sure there had been a single person in the car, a man.

Wyle Gaines. It had to be him.

"Mr. Declan just pulled up behind us," Rae said. "I didn't know he was coming over. Do you have more business?"

"We do," Everleigh responded. "He's going to have dinner with us, too. What do you think about pizza?"

"I want cheese pizza," she stated, sparking laughter.

"I already know that. I'll order a small one for you. I'm getting my usual veggie pizza."

Rae made a face. "Yucky."

Everleigh chuckled as she let her daughter out of the vehicle.

"Mr. Declan, I hope you like veggie pizza," Rae said when he entered the house behind them. "Mama does, but she's ordering me a cheese pizza."

"It doesn't matter to me," he replied with a smile. "I love any kind of pizza."

"Seriously, you can order whatever you like," Everleigh said.

"I'm good with the veggie pizza."

Rae entertained Declan by giving him the highlights of her day at school while they waited for the food to arrive.

"And Mandy...she was mean to me so I'm not her friend no more. I'm not gonna be mean back, but it makes me sad because God wants people to love each other."

"Yes, He does," he responded. "I know He's very proud of you, Rae."

"I'm proud of God, too." Rae got up and stalked into the kitchen. "Mama, if the food don't come soon, I'm gonna starve."

Everleigh glanced over at Declan, who was wearing a look of pure amusement on his face before he smiled down at her daughter. "Sweetie, it'll be here soon. There's a packet of sliced apples in the refrigerator. That should hold you over until the pizza comes."

"Thanks, Mama."

At the sound of the doorbell, Declan said, "Pizza's here." He gestured for Everleigh to let him get the food.

After they ate and Rae was settled for the evening, Everleigh and Declan spent most of the night searching for information on the victims and their families.

"James Ray Powell kidnapped, raped and murdered numerous young women during the 90s and possibly earlier," Everleigh stated. "After his arrest, he confessed to killing thirty women, but I'm sure the true number of his victims is higher."

"Lena Jones survived Powell. Back then, she was the only one willing to talk about her experience," Declan added from what he was reading. "She recounted how she woke up to find him standing over her. Lena stated that the only reason she was left alive was because of her roommate's boyfriend. They came home in the middle of the attack. He pulled Powell off Lena but wasn't able to stop him from escaping."

"I think you should talk to her."

"She's on my list," he responded. "She gave a couple interviews, testified in court. After that, Lena requested that she be left alone. There are no photos of her on record to protect her identity. That was the only way she'd agree to testify."

"Her face was blurred on television," Everleigh said. "I can certainly understand why she'd want privacy."

"There's a chance that she may not want to relive that period of her life, if and when we're able to locate her."

Everleigh picked up one of the throw pillows, hugging it close to her body. "I know, and we'll have no choice but to respect her wishes."

"I asked you this before, but do you think Wyle would take things this far?" Declan asked.

"I didn't initially," she murmured. "But now... I don't know."

"Nothing in his background makes him good for this. But when someone is desperate..."

"I guess I want it to be him because if it's not, the alternative is just too scary to think about." She held back a shudder. "Did you find anything else?"

He nodded. "As far as we know, this is the first victim," Declan said, handing over a file. "Hazel Claire Baisden. She died thirty-eight years ago, leaving behind three children, now ages forty-two and forty. The oldest son died in a car accident last year. Another is a New York police officer and the daughter is a schoolteacher in Los Angeles. I looked them all up."

"What are your impressions of her children?" Everleigh asked.

He thought for a moment, then said, "If it's not Wyle, then we're looking for someone who hasn't been able to move on from the loss of their loved one. But in this case, I honestly don't think it's either of Baisden's two surviving offspring."

Everleigh agreed. "The individual is most likely consumed with anger, probably have been in trouble with the law… I believe this is something that he or she has been planning for a long time. I hate to say it, but none of this sounds like Wyle. If he's involved at all, we're actually dealing with two people."

"I agree. Our assailant is organized and determined." Declan met her gaze. "This person is not going to give up. The shooting on campus was just practice."

Everleigh felt a shakiness in her limbs, her heartbeat raced and her adrenaline spiked. She got up and began to pace. "We have to find Wyle and whoever else is after me."

"I'm going to do everything I can."

She nodded. "I know you are. I just don't like feeling like I'm trapped. I'm not sure whom to trust."

"You don't have to worry about any of your students. They don't fit the profile," Declan said.

Everleigh was surprised to hear this. "You've already checked? I have well over a hundred students."

He nodded. "None of them are connected to any of the victims."

"That gives me some relief." Frowning in confusion, she added, "I just can't figure out Wyle's connection to all this. If there isn't one, then how did they find me?"

"With technology, people can find pretty much everything about a person."

"Which is exactly why I'm not on social media," Everleigh stated. "I find it too invasive. Still, I'm in no way connected to James Ray Powell."

"I can't figure that one out myself. Your mother must have told someone else outside of you and Wyle. Regardless of how they found out, they're a threat," Declan said. "That's why a cruiser will be parked out front throughout the night."

"Thank you for getting all that set up. I believe Rae and I will be fine, but having police parked outside the house makes me feel a bit more secure. However, my neighbors will most likely have some concerns."

"Who knows, they may feel more secure as well."

She grinned. "I hadn't thought about it that way. Our neighborhood's pretty quiet for the most part. Everyone parks in their garages—any cars in the driveway or parked out front belong to guests."

They stared at one another, and Everleigh felt her heart beating rapidly. She sat there trying to analyze what this was—a shared moment or just an awkward pause between them.

"I want you to know that you're not alone, Everleigh. We can get through anything you're facing—we can do it together."

She watched him, studying his expression. It was almost as if Declan could read her mind; he somehow knew exactly what she was feeling in that moment.

Declan smiled then, stirring something within her.

They let the conversation drift back to lighter topics for a bit, then he stood up a few minutes later and said, "I guess I'd better get out of here."

Everleigh walked him to the front door. "I'm really glad I don't have to deal with this by myself."

"I'll see you tomorrow."

When Declan left, Everleigh prepared for bed.

Rae was asleep in the middle of Everleigh's bed, so she made herself comfortable on a chaise lounge near the bedroom window. She turned her attention to her laptop screen. What little information Everleigh was able to find on Powell's family wasn't very helpful. She sat back, feeling overwhelmed. It saddened her that innocent members of his family had possibly died simply because of their association to the serial killer.

She wondered if Powell knew about the letters. Or if he would even care about what was happening? Everleigh found a documentary on him that could be streamed online. She knew so little about this man, so she fetched her headphones and settled in to watch it.

Narcissistic rage was a dangerous trait. James Ray Powell had a distorted worldview, an enlarged sense of entitlement and, because of deep-seated issues of rejection, he wanted to make people pay.

Powell grew up in a middle-class home, wanting for nothing in terms of material possessions and opportunities. He was shy and socially awkward. After Powell was arrested, police found a 100,000-word manifesto on his computer, documenting various personal slights and instances of rejection. Some were small and simply a part of growing up.

Powell described feeling jealous whenever so-called friends didn't pay attention to him as much in a group, and documented his struggles with self-esteem. He also described in detail the moments where he was rejected romantically, and was bullied in school.

As Everleigh watched the documentary, she noted that Powell never saw a problem as his fault. There didn't seem to be any moments of introspection or self-awareness. Instead, any and all blame was placed on others—women in particular. It was their rejecting him that had fed his anger.

It sickened her that this man had fathered her. That she was conceived out of a such a heinous criminal act. Everleigh thought about a former client who became pregnant as a result of rape. The woman worried if she'd ever be able to love her child.

Everleigh had told her that God was able to take the worst this world had to offer and make hope and new life. She reminded her client that God was able to create resurrection out of a murder on a cross. She assured the woman that God could create a beautiful child out of the violence she'd suffered. In this very moment, Everleigh had to take her own words to heart, and allow them to soothe and comfort her.

Powell himself was interviewed for the documentary, and he stated that he did everything he could to get women to like him, that their negative response to his efforts led to the destruction of his life and that by denying him the affection he desperately craved, they'd created the monster he became.

Studying his actions and body language, Everleigh watched Powell's attempts to ingratiate himself with the interviewer. She struggled with separating the man from his crimes. More than that was the shocking realization that his eyes, nose and mouth were mirrored in her own.

Her father, a serial killer, was looking at her each time she looked in a mirror.

When the documentary ended, Everleigh agreed with the diagnosis of narcissistic personality disorder. Powell displayed five of the nine established traits of narcissism. As for her, she felt nothing for him. No yearning to meet him. He was a dangerous man and not someone Everleigh wanted in her life or Rae's.

"Dear God, I know You and I haven't spent much time together since Britt died, but please don't let Powell find out about Rae and me," she whispered. "And keep us safe from whoever does know and wants to do us harm." Every time her husband had left for work, she'd prayed, asking God to keep him safe. She felt betrayed when Britt died saving a young boy. She'd been told that he was able to hand off the child, but found himself trapped.

Everleigh's eyes filled with tears as she thought of Britt alone in that burning house. She was proud of his heroic efforts, but there was a part of her that was angry that he hadn't thought of his own safety. Guilt seeped from her pores because of it.

She swiped at her eyes. "I just want all this to end. And everybody responsible—I want them found and locked up. We've been through enough, God."

FIVE

Declan decided not to leave Angel Island right away. Despite the cruiser outside the house, he felt the need to see for himself that Everleigh and Rae were safe, as he'd promised. He sat there for nearly two hours, but found nothing unusual and no one lurking around the neighborhood.

The island had always been a pretty little coastal town, and was growing in popularity. One of the main attractions was the low crime rate, along with the picturesque beaches, quaint neighborhoods and unique boutiques downtown. It was in close proximity to Hilton Head and Polk Island.

He paused to have a conversation with the police officer guarding the house before heading back to Charleston.

Once he was home, Declan checked on Everleigh and Rae via text.

Declan: Hey, it's me. How are things?

Everleigh: We're good. About to call it a night. Police are outside.

Declan: See you tomorrow.

Everleigh: Thx again.

Declan walked into his family room and sat down on the leather sofa. He eyed the jigsaw puzzle he'd started on a few days ago. He often turned to puzzles for stress relief.

He sat down and began putting the pieces together, but his mind wasn't on the puzzle—he was thinking of Everleigh.

There was an undeniable connection building between them, forcing him to concede the truth—he couldn't ignore the deep feelings he was developing for Everleigh. They weren't going away anytime soon.

Declan hadn't looked forward to their evening coming to an end. He'd enjoyed spending time with her and Rae. Everleigh possessed a warm, loving spirit and was always smiling. He loved her humor and the sense of freedom she seemed to have in her life, even in her current situation. But as strong as his attraction was to her, Declan would never act on those feelings.

With Everleigh at the forefront of his mind, he couldn't fully concentrate on the puzzle so he gave up for the night.

Declan made his way to the second level, where his bedroom was located.

He lay in bed thinking about Everleigh and the feelings she ignited in him. Although she was a widow, he could tell that in her heart, she was still very much a married woman. Declan was here to do a job, so he had no choice but to wrangle in his emotions.

"Somehow she knew she was being followed," he said. "Look, we're really gonna have be careful. She's talking to the cops."

"H-How do you kno…kn-know? The shots on campus could've come from a-anybody… and nobody was hit."

"She works with a detective or criminologist—the way I figure it, she must've told him about the letter. He followed her home tonight and then stayed for a while. I left when a cop arrived. Don't know if the dude left. He might still be there."

"Maybe they're d-dating," his brother said. "She's not a bad looker."

Shrugging in nonchalance, he uttered, "Don't matter to me. If he gets in the way, we'll just get rid of him, too."

"The daughter was in the car. I n-never agreed to anything about k-killing a child. That little g-girl is innocent."

Fury spread through him. "That girl has Powell's blood running through her veins. We said we were gonna take out the entire bloodline."

His words were met with silence. After a moment passed, he said, "Look, I don't like the idea of hurting a little kid, either, but she is his future."

"I don't like it," his brother responded.

"The decision's already been made. We're keeping to the plan."

"Whatever, man... I hate talking to you wh-when you're like this."

"I'm just following the plan," he repeated. "You should do the same."

Everleigh sat in her home office munching on a dill-pickle spear. As she chewed, her mind turned to her upcoming online lecture on borderline personality disorder, or BPD. In her career as a psychotherapist, she'd treated several people with BPD.

People suffering from the disorder experienced an intense fear of abandonment, instability, inappropriate anger, impulsiveness and frequent mood swings. There were several serial killers diagnosed with BPD. Powell was a narcissist. He didn't have this disorder.

Her doorbell camera app popped open on her screen.

It was Declan. He'd mentioned he might come by when they spoke earlier.

She walked up to the front door and opened it. "Hey… come on in."

"I sent you a text that I was on my way. I figured you were still in class."

She glanced up at Declan and smiled. "Done for the day. Are you hungry? I made a sandwich for Rae, but she wanted a hot dog."

"Sure," he responded, following her into the kitchen.

Everleigh retrieved the sandwich from the refrigerator and placed it on a plate with a pickle and some chips. "For some reason, I didn't think you had a class today."

She put it on the table in front of Declan.

"I don't, but I'm meeting with a student in an hour. I wanted to check on you and Rae first."

"We're fine," Everleigh responded, while trying to sound calmer than she actually felt. "Thankfully, everything has been quiet so far."

They settled in across the table from each other.

"I watched a documentary on Powell last night," she announced.

Declan eyed her. "Thoughts?"

"I'm glad he's in prison."

"He was given life without parole."

"He deserves it," she replied. "He's not repentant at all. He believes the victims got what *they* deserved. He actually said that women created the monster in him."

"People like him don't accept responsibility for their actions."

"You're right."

"Had you looked him up before now?" Declan asked.

"No, not until last night." She gave a slight shrug. "I don't know why I did it. It wasn't out of any special *feel-*

ings toward him. That documentary confirmed one thing for me. I definitely don't want him in our lives. However, I really don't think it'll be much of a problem if he does find out. The one thing that came across the documentary and his interviews—James Ray Powell doesn't care about anyone other than himself."

Declan and Everleigh sat there talking for the next twenty minutes. He always enjoyed their conversations outside of the investigation.

"I'd love to hear your perspective on something," she said. "There's a scripture in Exodus about God punishing the children and their children for the sin of the parents to the third and fourth generations. Do you believe in intergenerational punishment for sin?"

He responded almost instantly, "Deuteronomy 24:16 says 'The fathers shall not be put to death for the children, neither shall the children put to death for the fathers: every man shall be put to death for his own sin.' Also, Ezekiel 18 is very clear on this. Guilt belongs to the person who sinned, not their family."

"Whoever is trying to kill me obviously believes otherwise," Everleigh said. "I know there's been trauma, but this is also misplaced anger."

"They're bound to make a mistake, and then we'll catch them."

She nodded in agreement. "That's what I keep telling myself. But then I think about the members of Powell's family—the ones who didn't deserve to die just because they were related to him. Whoever is doing this is no better than the man he despises."

Everleigh glanced down at her watch. "I guess I'd better get back to the computer. I have one more class."

"How's it going?"

"Teaching via video is a little weird, but my students are game for it and I don't mind too much. If you don't have anything else to do, feel free to hang out." Her smile was warm and inviting.

"Sure. I'd like that."

Everleigh appeared more relaxed around him than she had before. He hadn't expected to be awestruck by her beauty and warmth, which he found incredibly inviting. She had a way of looking elegant in everything she wore; from a suit, to a pair of jeans and a sweater. Declan liked to see her with her hair down, but whenever she was on campus, Everleigh kept her glossy tresses secured in a ponytail or bun. This awareness of her, even the unfamiliar urge Declan had to stare at her, was unlike him. It unsettled him whenever he was in her presence. He wasn't just attracted to her physical beauty; he was attracted to her mind. Declan was a man of faith and he liked that it was something they had in common.

At the end of her class, she rejoined him in the family room.

"Do you have any plans for the weekend after next?" he asked.

Everleigh shook her head. "What's up?"

"I'd like to take you and your daughter to the annual Christmas Festival on Polk Island. But only if there's no other incidents."

She grinned. "Sounds wonderful. Rae would love something like that, but I won't mention it until I know that we're going. Thank you for thinking of us, Declan. I've heard a lot about Polk Island but we haven't gone over there yet."

"You'd love it. It's a lot like Angel Island, but lots of tourists. However, it's very family-oriented."

"There will be rides, games and lots of other attractions."

"That's perfect. She doesn't care much for Ferris wheel-type rides, but if they have a merry-go-round, she'd be okay with that."

"There's a lot to see in Charleston, too," Declan said.

"Maybe you can show me around," Everleigh murmured.

"Definitely."

"This feels nice," she said after a moment. "This is the first time I've felt pretty normal since this whole nightmare started."

"I'm glad. Maybe after today, they might give up."

"That would be wonderful, Declan, but I'm sure you know better than that. They're too invested now."

Everleigh was right. He didn't believe the assailant had given up on killing her. That was why he wanted to keep her close by. Or so he told himself. That all of this was about keeping Everleigh and Rae safe from harm.

He and Everleigh had grown closer—things were good between them and Declan never wanted to tamper with that.

SIX

Everleigh was up early the next morning because she hadn't slept well during the night. Every couple of hours or so, she'd ease out of bed to see if the police vehicle was still parked outside. She also checked for any unfamiliar cars in the neighborhood. Everything looked normal, but Everleigh couldn't afford to let down her guard.

She returned to bed and eased under the covers next to Rae, hoping to catch one more hour of sleep before starting her day.

An image of Declan's handsome face swam before her, along with the unexpected impact of his beautiful dark eyes.

Everleigh was a widow. She still mourned her husband. She definitely wasn't interested in dating, but she welcomed his friendship. She hadn't really made any friends locally, focusing instead on helping Rae settle in and excelling at her new job at the university.

Sleep continued to elude her so Everleigh gave up. She got out of bed and padded to the shower.

She dressed quickly without disturbing Rae and went downstairs to the kitchen.

Everleigh had just finished making breakfast when she received a text from another member of the psychology faculty. Robin Rutledge and her husband lived nearby. Everleigh didn't know her well, but she knew they were expecting their first child. She responded quickly and headed to the front of her house.

"I thought you might want to check out this new textbook on abnormal psychology," Robin said when she arrived. "Fall semester next year, I'll be teaching parapsychology. I saw that you'll be teaching Abnormal Psychology Two."

They taught classes on parapsychology here? That surprised her a bit. Everleigh had no desire to explore this area of psychology, which involved psychic phenomena such as telepathy and telekinesis. She accepted the book, then said, "Thanks."

"I noticed the police car out front. Everleigh, is someone really after you?"

After the shooting, Everleigh had had to explain to her department head what was going on. She'd asked that the word be spread quietly among other faculty members.

"We're thinking it might this guy that befriended my mom—he got very upset with me when I refused to sell him the house. I knew it the moment I met him that he was manipulating her."

"Is there anything I can do?" Robin asked.

"Just be on the lookout for strangers in the neighborhood."

"I'll let my husband know as well. He gets up all times of the night to walk the dog."

"Thank you, Robin."

Placing her hand on her swollen belly, the other woman added, "I'll be glad when this little one gets here."

"You don't have much longer."

"Six weeks."

There was a time when Everleigh thought she'd expand

her family, but Britt's death changed that for her. She was grateful to have her daughter, but she'd never wished for Rae to grow up an only child. Perhaps the Lord had other plans.

After Robin left, Everleigh prepared a plate and a large cup of coffee, then took it outside. The night before there had been a male officer.

"There must have been a shift change," she said. "I was expecting to see the officer that was here all night."

"Yes ma'am. I'll be here until three o'clock."

"Thank you for your service and especially for making sure my daughter and I are safe."

"It's my duty, ma'am." Accepting the food and coffee, she added, "Thank you for this. It smells delicious."

"Declan told me that there will be someone patrolling the area at night. I wasn't sure there would be anyone here during the day. I don't recall seeing anyone out here yesterday"

"There was a special duty officer here. They were in plain clothes and not in a cruiser."

She nodded in understanding. "I don't suppose there has been any movement in the investigation." It was a statement rather than a question.

"Well," Everleigh continued, "If you need anything, please just ring the doorbell."

The officer smiled. "Thank you, ma'am."

Back inside, Everleigh turned on the alarm.

She loved the design of her house and the amazing view of the ocean from her kitchen, sunroom and patio. Everleigh had fallen in love with the home the first time the Realtor had brought her to see it.

She also had a view of the garden that they'd planted. The only thing missing out back on the sprawling deck was an outdoor kitchen. Everleigh wanted to have one built before the summer. She enjoyed grilling when the weather was warm.

Everleigh turned away from the window.

Her eyes traveled from the faux-finished stucco walls to the hand-painted breakfast table and chairs to the plush overstuffed sofa. She glanced down at the glossy hardwood flooring throughout the main level.

An hour later, Everleigh heard movement upstairs and searched out Rae. She found Rae in own bedroom with a book.

"Good morning, sweetie. What are you reading?" she whispered against her cheek.

"Umm… I'm just looking at the pictures. Will you read it to me?"

"How about you read it to me after breakfast?" she responded. "I made pancakes."

Nodding, Rae said, "Okay, but you have to help me."

"I'd be happy to, sweetie. You want to help me make the scrambled eggs?"

"I do. Yay!"

"Go wash your face and I'll get your apron," Everleigh said.

"I want my chief hat, too."

She laughed. "You mean your chef hat."

"I'm so happy," Rae announced when she walked into the kitchen.

Everleigh smiled. "So am I."

"Mama, why are you happy?"

Rae's question caught her off guard. She presented herself as if she didn't have a care in the world, when she was wavering somewhere between fear and anger. But somehow Rae was picking up on positivity Everleigh hadn't noticed in herself, too. "Because I have you," she responded.

"Because I have my life, a job I really like… What about you? Why are you so happy?"

"Because you're my mama. And because my daddy and Grandma is watching over us in heaven."

"That's a great reason to be happy." Rae's happiness mattered to Everleigh.

"I'm also happy because it's gonna be Christmas."

She helped her daughter with her apron. "We can't forget that, huh?"

Rae shook her head. She planted herself on a stool. "Mama, it's gonna be a good one. You'll see."

"I know it will," Everleigh said. "Because I get to spend it with you."

She placed a plastic bowl in front of her daughter and handed her a whisk.

"Did you see the policeman outside our house?" Rae asked. "I saw him from the window upstairs. I think he was tired and he needed a nap."

She released the breath she'd been holding, grateful that her daughter didn't seem fazed by a police cruiser parked outside. "It's a woman officer." Everleigh retrieved the eggs and milk from the refrigerator.

"We should take her some food. She might be hungry."

"I already did."

"She might still want some pancakes," Rae said.

Smiling, Everleigh observed her daughter as she cracked three eggs into the bowl. Then she poured milk into a measuring cup and handed it to Rae. "You're so much like your daddy. He was always so thoughtful. He'd put the needs of others before his own. He was a wonderful man."

"Grandma told me that Daddy will always live in my heart."

"She was absolutely right about that," she responded. "And so will Grandma. She will live in our hearts forever."

"Mama, I like Mr. Declan. Do *you* like him?" Rae asked as she whisked the contents in the bowl into a creamy mixture.

"Yes," she answered. "He's a really nice man."

"A girl in my class has two daddies," her daughter said. "Do you think one day I'll get another one?"

Stunned by the question, Everleigh asked, "How would you feel about that?"

Rae shrugged. "I don't know. I guess it'll be good."

"Right now, we're just going to focus on getting settled in this house," she said, pouring the egg mixture into a frying pan. "It's almost Christmas and we haven't put out any decorations yet." She thought it best to try to keep things as normal as possible for Rae.

"Is that why I'm not going to school again?"

"No, that's not the reason. I spoke with your teacher and we're going to try something new. You're going to be able to stay home but you'll be able to see everyone through the computer."

"Why?"

"We're trying it out. Remember, I'm even trying it with my class."

"But why?"

"It's a test run, Rae. That's all."

After breakfast, Everleigh set up her personal laptop. "See, there's your teacher…"

She waved, then said, "Everybody's at school but me."

"Okay, I need you to pay attention, sweetie."

This was the second day and she had already run out of excuses. Everleigh had no idea how much longer she would be able to keep Rae in the dark.

The weather became gloomy later that evening.

Thick, black clouds trundled in over the city. Lightning

erupted as heavy layers of cold rain poured down, turning the sidewalks and streets to puddles. The temperature dropped as gusts of wind swept in, foreshadowing an early winter storm.

Everleigh turned away from the window. She walked over to the sofa and sat down beside her daughter.

"I don't like when it rains. The thunder is scary," the little girl said.

She wrapped an arm around Rae. "I know, sweetie. But there's nothing for you to be afraid of—it's only rain."

Outside, the wind continued to shriek, and the rain poured down as if it had a point to make.

Truthfully, Everleigh didn't like bad weather, either, but she wasn't fearful of rainstorms.

"Why don't we get ready for bed?"

"Mama, come with me."

Together, they went through the house checking the windows and the doors. Everleigh was careful not to trigger the alarm. Then they retired to her bedroom.

She checked her messages while Rae took a bath. When the lights flickered, Everleigh pulled out a flashlight from a drawer in the nightstand. She also pulled out a couple of emergency candles and a lighter.

"Mama…"

"I'm coming, sweetie."

Everleigh crossed the room in quick strides.

She helped Rae dry off with a fluffy towel. "You smell like bubble gum."

Rae giggled. "*Strawberry* bubble gum."

After her daughter was settled in bed, Everleigh turned on the television. "The lightning and thunder have stopped, so we can watch a little TV."

"Yay!"

Her daughter fell asleep within the hour, leaving her

to finish the animated movie they were watching alone. Everleigh went downstairs to get a bottle of water when it ended. Before going back to her bedroom, she stole a peek out the living room window.

A police cruiser slowed as it passed her house. The forty-eight-hour watch was over, so they were no longer camping outside the house but drove by several times throughout the night.

She suddenly had disturbing quakes in her body, but didn't fully understand why. Everleigh did one more walk-through for her own peace of mind.

There was a car parked at the corner, but other than that, she didn't notice anything or anyone. All the Tasers in her home were fully charged; there were items she could use to fend off an attacker hidden throughout and a very nice bat under the sofa and another one under her bed.

Everleigh had just slid under the covers when her phone started to vibrate.

It was Declan.

"Hey, did you get any rain in Charleston?" she asked when she answered, keeping her voice low so as to not disturb Rae.

"It was pouring down earlier. I think it's down to a drizzle now. Did I call at a bad time?"

She eased out of bed and made her way quietly over to the chaise. "No, your timing's perfect."

"I wanted to check in with you before calling it a night," Declan said. "Make sure everything is fine. I know the police are doing drive-bys every thirty minutes or so."

"All is well over here. Windows and doors are secured, the alarm is on..."

"Good."

"Don't you dare drive to the island to check on us," Everleigh said with a chuckle.

"Wow. You're getting to know me pretty well."

"Seriously, stay home. We're fine." She didn't want Declan going out of his way for them—he'd already done enough and she was grateful.

"I'm a phone call away," he said. "I don't care about the time. Seriously, call or text if you need me."

"I will, Declan."

"How is my little friend?"

"Sleeping soundly," Everleigh responded. "She doesn't like storms so she had a little anxiety earlier."

"I won't keep you."

"Thanks so much for calling."

"Do you mind if I come to the house tomorrow after work?" he asked.

"Rae and I would love to see you." Everleigh enjoyed Declan's company.

When they hung up, she glanced down at her wedding rings. "Britt, I miss you so much. Rae misses you, too." She paused a moment to gather her thoughts. "I really wish you were here. Someone wants to harm us... You'd know exactly what to do."

An image of Declan formed in her head.

"This guy...his name is Declan. He's been looking into this threat, so I don't have to deal with it alone."

Everleigh released a sigh. "Oh, Britt... I have to let you go."

She peeked out her window, then got up and headed back to bed. She needed to get some sleep. Morning would come quickly.

He let out an impatient sigh. They had been parked on that corner for nearly an hour.

"Man, what's w-wrong witcha?" his brother asked. "You

over there huffin' and puff…puffin' like you itching to blow s-something down."

"We could go in there and take care of them right now. What we out here waiting for?"

"W-We have to be careful, man."

"Ain't nobody watching the house anymore," he said.

"I don't g-guess you haven't noticed the cop that d-drives by every thirty minutes. She also upgraded her security system."

"How do you know?"

"When I came by here the other d-day, I saw the van pa…parked out front," his brother responded.

He laughed out loud. "That won't stop us."

Just then a police car turned on the street.

They ducked down in their seats.

"That's the second time that cop done come down this street. You see how he slows down when he gets to her house. Let's get out of here," he said when the cruiser disappeared.

"I don't have a good f-feelin' about this, man."

Muttering a string of profanity, he started the car. "I'ma listen to you this time. But as soon as I get the chance, I'm taking them out."

"I can't believe that you haven't eaten at Vanny's Place before," Declan said as they pored over a couple of menus, Everleigh had retrieved from a drawer in the kitchen. "It's an Angel Island staple."

"It was on my list to try," Everleigh responded. "We just hadn't gotten around to doing so."

"Do they have macaroni and cheese?" Rae asked from where she was seated on the couch in the family room.

"They do," he answered. "And it's delicious."

"I hope it's as good as Grandma's. She makes the best. Even better than Mama."

Declan swallowed his amusement. "Oh."

Everleigh laughed. "She's right. Mine doesn't compare to my mother's mac and cheese. She would never tell me her secret ingredient. One day Rae and I will figure it out, though."

She glanced down at the menu, then said, "So what do you recommend we try?"

"The rigatoni with shrimp, mushrooms and peppers is one of my favorites," he said. "Another is the liver and onions."

"Do they have chicken?" Rae asked. "I like fried chicken."

Everleigh surveyed the menu. "They have it, sweetie. You can get a drumstick with mac and cheese and broccoli."

"Yay. That's what I want. And lemonade."

Declan tried not to stare at Everleigh while they waited for their food to be delivered. She was stunning. "Oh, I checked up on Gaines and looks like he moved out of his place. His neighbor said Wyle told him that he had to leave town and wasn't sure when he'd be back."

"I'd bet money that he's in Charleston," she responded.

Fifteen minutes later, the food had been delivered and they sat around the dining room table.

Everleigh blessed the food before they sampled their meals.

"Declan, everything smells delicious."

Fork in hand, he replied, "Wait until you taste it."

"Do you have any kids?" Rae asked.

"No, I haven't been blessed in finding a wife yet," he responded. "But I hope to have some one day."

"Oh," the little girl murmured.

She sounded so disappointed, Declan thought to himself.

"She doesn't have a lot of friends," Everleigh explained.

"I'm not a kid, but I'd love to have you as a friend," he said. "You and your mom both."

Rae beamed. "Yay. I like friends."

Thank you, Everleigh mouthed to him.

"Did you move here because of the job?"

Nodding, she replied, "I'd made up my mind to relocate but I wasn't sure where. Then the offer came to teach... so here we are. What about you. Is Charleston where you grew up?"

"No, I'm originally from Columbia. I ended up here for the job, too."

"What do you do for fun?" she asked.

"I love spending time at the beach or a lake pretty much anywhere."

"You're a water baby..." Everleigh said. "That's what my mother used to call people who love being around water."

Declan chuckled. "Yeah that's me—a true water baby."

Pointing to the macaroni and cheese, Rae stated, "Mama, you gotta try it. It tastes almost like Grandma's."

Everleigh stuck a forkful into her mouth. "Oh, my goodness. This is delicious. You're right. It *does* taste like hers."

"Did your mom put cayenne pepper in hers?" Declan asked.

"That's it." She looked at him. "How did you know?"

"I asked the chef after the first time I had it. She told me that she uses Colby, cheddar, Monterey Jack cheese and cayenne pepper."

"We make ours with all those—I just never knew about the cayenne pepper. Mystery solved."

"We make a great team," he replied.

To Declan's delight, she agreed.

"Thank you both for having pity on me," he said after

wiping his mouth on a paper napkin. "I didn't want to eat alone."

"Mr. Declan, you don't have to eat by yourself," Rae responded. "You can eat at our house all the time, can't he, Mama."

She smiled. "You heard my daughter. Feel free to join us when you can."

Breaking into a grin, he said, "Don't play… I just might take you up on that."

"We welcome the company."

Her words touched Declan to the core.

SEVEN

After dinner, Rae wrangled the adults into watching a Disney movie with her.

"You have gone above and beyond the call of duty, Declan," Everleigh said appreciatively. "And you've been such a good sport about it."

"I enjoy spending time with you and Rae. She reminds me so much of my great-niece Halle."

"As soon as I get Rae settled for the evening, we can discuss your findings if you don't mind sticking around," Everleigh whispered. She didn't want her daughter overhearing that part of their conversation.

"I'm good," Declan responded. "I don't have any other plans for the evening."

"You've been such a good friend to us. Rae's been through a lot to be so young. The loss of her father and then her grandmother…"

"She's not the only one. You also suffered those losses."

Everleigh nodded. "This is true. It's just that she's a little girl."

"Does Rae talk about her father much?" Declan asked.

"Yes, she does. When she brings him up, she talks about him being in Heaven with God. It's the same with my mom, too. Rae truly believes that her father and grandmother are with the Lord. It seems to give her a measure of peace."

"And you?"

"It's the same for me," Everleigh replied. "My husband loved God—so did my mother. I am confident that they will spend eternity with Him."

She allowed Rae to watch one of her favorite cartoons before announcing, "Time for bed. C'mon, let's go upstairs."

"Okay." She glanced over at Declan and smiled.

"G'night, little lady," he said to Rae.

Giggling, she replied, "Good night Mr. Declan. I hope you'll still be here when I wake up in the morning."

Everleigh hoped he didn't hear her sudden intake of breath. Her daughter had no idea the impact of her words. Rae liked Declan and it was possible that she'd begun to see him as a father figure.

She wasn't sure how she felt about this. Everleigh tabled the thought for now. They had more pressing matters to contend with, like finding Wyle. She hoped he was able to fill in some of the blanks.

Throughout the evening, Declan could hardly keep his eyes off Everleigh. He gave himself a mental shake and told himself that he needed to rein in his emotions.

From outward appearances, Everleigh looked fragile, but he knew she possessed a quiet strength—one of the many qualities that drew him to her, despite his resolve to keep their relationship platonic. She was the only woman Declan had felt connected to in a long time—she made him feel things that had been long forgotten.

"Baby girl is all settled in bed," Everleigh announced, walking briskly into the family room. She sat down on the sofa.

"I checked in with the police department on the island. There's been a car with Maryland tags in your neighborhood a few times. They could be visiting someone on your street."

"That's most likely the reason," Everleigh said. "If they were there for us, I'm sure we would've known by now. It's not Wyle. His drives a BMW and has Georgia tags."

"Well, tonight I'll probably drive around and do my own surveillance."

"Declan, you don't have to do that," she quickly interjected. "That's too much."

"I told you that nothing was going to happen to you and Rae on my watch. I meant that."

"My neighbors do have guests from time to time. I don't want to become paranoid. I refuse to live my life that way."

"I agree with you, but you have to remain vigilant. Don't let your guard down. If you feel like something's not right, we need to check it out."

"I just don't want you to start feeling as if you're chasing your tail."

"We've established that there is a valid threat against you and Rae," he responded. "The letter, the campus shooting and that SUV that followed you…"

"I guess I'm wavering in denial."

"I'm still looking for Lena Jones."

"She's most likely still in hiding," Everleigh said. "I don't blame her."

"At least there haven't been any more deaths in the Powell family," Declan stated. "At least none that we know about."

"And nothing to connect the three that were found."

He leaned forward, resting his elbows on his knees. "Tell me everything you know about Wyle and your mother's relationship."

"They worked together at the hospital—different departments," Everleigh said. "They would have lunch together and that soon progressed to dinners, the theater and even church."

"Was his interest in her romantic?"

"She said it wasn't—that they were just good friends. They used to talk on the phone for hours. They had similar interests. At least Wyle made her believe that they did. He knew about my mom's cancer before she told me. My suspicions grew when he began taking an interest in her finances."

"What exactly did he want to know?" Declan asked.

"She sought his advice about investments and stocks. I walked in one day while they were discussing it. My mom was about to hand over five thousand dollars for him to invest—I don't know in what, but I put a stop to it right then and there. I could tell Wyle wasn't pleased. I knew that he wasn't to be trusted."

"He's an amateur, so he's bound to make a mistake. I intend to be around when he does." Declan stood up. "I guess I'd better get out of here. I want to do a little surveillance of my own."

They bid each other good-night, and Declan whistled softly as he made his way to his car.

Forty-five minutes later, he was cruising past Everleigh's house with a coffee in a to-go cup. There were no cars on the street. No signs of anyone walking around.

He was grateful everything was quiet.

Declan liked that Everleigh wasn't the type to panic without reason, but he hoped she wouldn't be naive enough to think the danger had passed. There wasn't any record of violence in Wyle's background, but he had to consider that the man just hadn't gotten caught. Perhaps he was waiting for the perfect opportunity to make his move.

* * *

Everleigh woke with a start. She sat up, looking around in the dark and listening.

She picked up her tablet and checked the security cameras. Some of the tension in her shoulders melted away when she saw a police cruiser drive by.

Just as Everleigh was about to lie back down, the alarm began emitting the words, "Glass break."

"Mama," Rae shouted, startling awake.

"Honey, it's okay." She picked her up and said, "Barbie's in trouble." Rushing into Rae's room with her daughter in her arms, she asked, "You remember what you're supposed to do, right?"

The little girl nodded, hurried into the closet and hid inside the toy chest.

Everleigh armed herself with the Taser from her nightstand and waited a few minutes in the hallway before descending the stairs. Rae was supposed to call 911 and leave the phone on. There was an officer already in the neighborhood so it shouldn't be a long wait for help to arrive.

She didn't hear any movement—only deafening silence.

When she glimpsed an officer approaching the door, Everleigh rushed down the stairs to open it.

She sagged with relief. "My alarm just reported a glass break. I decided to wait for you before I investigate. I had my daughter hide. She's the one who called 911."

"That was a wise choice, ma'am," he said. "You stay in here and I'll check."

Everleigh nodded.

When the officer returned, he told her, "Someone threw a rock and it hit one of the windows in the back. It's gonna need replacing. Might've been some kids playing around. We try to keep them off the beach this late at night…"

"You didn't see anybody then?" she asked.

"No, ma'am."

"Thank you for checking—I'm relieved that it's nothing more," Everleigh said. "My little girl is hiding so I'd better go up and assure her that we're safe."

He smiled. "Yes, ma'am. I'll be right out front for the rest of the night. I'll keep checking the back of your house as well, but I suggest you get some motion lights."

"I agree."

After locking the door, she hurried up the stairs. "Rae, honey. Come on out. Everything is okay."

"Mama, did someone try to—"

"No," Everleigh interjected. "Some kids were throwing rocks and one hit our window. The police officer came and checked everything. He said he's going to keep watch for the rest of the night. There's nothing to worry about, sweetie."

"I did everything you told me to do."

"You did a great job. I'm so proud of you."

"Can we go back to bed now?" Rae asked.

Everleigh gave a nervous chuckle. "We sure can, sweetie."

The edges of night rolled back, giving the sun entrance. She lay in bed, still unable to fall asleep. Her daughter hadn't had a problem, however.

She eased out of bed and crept over to the window. The cruiser was outside.

Everleigh showered. She dressed in a pair of gray jeans and a thick burgundy sweater. She combed her hair, then pulled it into a messy bun.

Downstairs, she made herself a cup of tea, then sat down in the family room. Everleigh wrapped herself in the warmth of a throw.

She didn't realize that she'd fallen asleep until she woke up to Rae cuddling beside her on the sofa.

"Sweetie, what are you doing up so early?"

"I woke up and you weren't there. I came looking for you."

Everleigh placed an arm around Rae. "You want to go back up to bed? I'll go with you."

"I wanna stay down here with you."

Her internal clock went off two hours later, waking Everleigh.

"It's time to get moving, Rae. I'll make breakfast while you get dressed."

"Okay, Mama," Rae murmured, rubbing her eyes and yawning. "Is the test over? Do I get to go to school today?"

"No, because it's Saturday, sweetie."

"I can't wait until Monday. Then I'll see my friends at school."

"Lord, please let this be over soon," Everleigh prayed, when Rae went upstairs to her room They would soon take a break for the holidays and it couldn't come quick enough for her.

EIGHT

Everleigh took one look at Declan's face when he arrived Monday afternoon and asked, "What happened? I can tell by your expression that something's wrong."

"Powell's niece was found dead in Maryland on the same day someone shot at you. Around the same time, actually."

She considered his words. "So are you thinking that we were wrong? Or that this was a coordinated attack?"

"It's possible that Wyle was the shooter on campus, trying to scare you. But even if that's the case, there *is* an assailant targeting Powell's family," Declan responded. "I have to say that this investigation is becoming more convoluted by the minute."

Massaging her forehead, Everleigh said, "I don't know what to think right now."

"We have to seriously consider that if Wyle Gaines is involved, he's somehow connected to another assailant."

"How was she killed? Powell's niece."

"She was shot twice. But no letter was found at the crime scene. The police are now looking to determine if all the murders are connected because of the victims' relationship to Powell. They're considering that there's a serial killer targeting the family but need some solid evidence."

"Declan, maybe we're overreacting about all of this," Everleigh said. "If someone other than Wyle was really after me, why haven't they made a move? They've had several opportunities to do so."

She didn't want to believe that a serial killer was targeting her and Rae.

"I don't think we're wrong," he answered. "Powell's relatives are not dying of natural causes. There is a real threat out there."

A chill snaked down her spine. "I knew you were going to say that."

"I pray I'm wrong, but I don't think that I am, Everleigh."

"In the meantime, I don't want to risk any of the students or other staff members getting harmed. There are only a couple days left before the holiday break. If this isn't resolved, I think it's best that I ask for a leave of absence until this is settled. Rae has another week but I'm keeping her home with me."

"I know you don't like it, but this is a really good idea," Declan responded.

She sat down to make the necessary phone calls. Declan leaned back in his chair and did some work on his phone.

Two calls later, she said, "They're emailing me the paperwork."

"That's good to hear."

"I already spoke to Rae's teacher, too. She won't be going back to school until I know that we're safe."

"I'm sorry, Everleigh."

"You don't have to apologize. It's not your fault. I just hope you find whoever is responsible. I don't want them controlling my life like this."

"I hope you know that I'm doing everything I can."

She smiled softly at him. "I don't doubt that. I don't guess you know about the little scare we had last night."

His expression quickly turned to one of concern. "What happened?"

"Someone was throwing rocks and one hit my window," she stated. "It set the alarm off. There was an officer in the neighborhood… I think his last name was Lee. He checked inside and around the back." Everleigh shrugged. "I don't think it was really anything, but I had Rae hide in her closet."

"Do you really believe that this was yet another random incident?" Declan asked.

She shook her head. "Robin's husband installed some motion lights in the back of the house this morning. The rock—that sounds more like Wyle. Psychological torture—I can see him doing something like this. He's more into the head games."

"I'd like to pin all this on Wyle, but we can't dismiss what's happening to the people related to Powell," he said. "We can't definitively prove that the deaths are all related yet, but my instincts tell me they are."

"I'd rather be cautious, trust me. I won't risk my daughter's safety. I hope you find Wyle soon. I'd like to know his connection in all this."

"The thing that bothers me most is that there haven't been any letters found with any of the victims. It doesn't make sense to only send a letter to you and not the others."

"It's possible they threw them away," she responded. "I almost threw mine away, but it felt real, so that's why I took it to you. They could've easily dismissed it."

"I thought about that, especially since they could've previously experienced harassment about because of their relationship to Powell. There was an interview with his sister. She received death threats for months right after he was arrested. She said her parents received them as well. Just so you know, I sent copies of the letter to all the investigators."

"I hope it helps them." Everleigh folded her arms across her chest. "Any updates on Wyle?"

"He's officially a person of interest now. If he's in Charleston, we will find out soon."

"Good," she replied. "It's time we get answers."

Everleigh turned off her computer monitor after her noon class ended. She didn't mind teaching virtually, though she'd enjoy it more under different circumstances. Part of it was having to deal with Rae.

"Mama, I'm bored," her daughter said from the doorway. "I wanna go outside."

"Honey, I'm sorry, but you can't. We need to stay inside the house."

"Why?"

"It's too cold outside."

"No, it's not."

"Rae, I'm not going to argue with you about this. I said no and I mean it."

Everleigh was a woman who loved the outdoors. She wasn't happy being a prisoner in her own home. Clearly, Rae wasn't happy with the changes, either.

"Why don't I make us some lunch," she offered, getting up from her desk.

In the kitchen, Everleigh made a peanut-butter-and-jelly sandwich for Rae and a salad for herself.

A few minutes later, she announced, "Your lunch is on the table."

"Yes, ma'am," Rae responded. "I'm still bored."

They sat down at the breakfast table to eat. "I know

you are, but I have an idea. Why don't you work on your sight words?"

"You put them all over my room. It's crowded now."

She hid a smile. "I placed them there to help you recognize the words."

"I know, but my room is crowded."

Rae was irritable and her mood wasn't likely to improve until she got her way.

And that wasn't happening.

"Guess who's coming over for dinner?" Everleigh said, hoping this would cheer up Rae. They hadn't been able to find any common ground, so she was looking forward to having a conversation with no bickering.

"Mr. Declan?"

"Yes, and he's bringing dinner."

Her daughter's face lit up like a star on top of the tree. "Yay!"

Everleigh eyed Rae. Her attitude had completely shifted at the mention of Declan. It stayed that way for the rest of the afternoon. She didn't even have to ask her daughter more than once to clean up her toys.

It was a few minutes after six when Declan arrived. Everleigh was just as thrilled to see him as her daughter was.

"I brought dinner as promised," he said.

"Thank you," she responded. "You didn't have to do that, but it's much appreciated."

Afterward, he took them out for a drive. She'd told him earlier about Rae wanting to get out of the house.

She looked out the passenger side window at the Christmas decorations highlighting each shop as they rode through the downtown area. The streetlights were decorated with holly, star-shaped lights and red velvet ribbons. In the middle of Center Square, a tall, beautifully decorated tree held court.

Declan parked the car and they got out for a closer look.

"Mama, look at the angel on top. She's so pretty."

"Yes, she is," Everleigh responded.

They stopped at a vendor selling roasted chestnuts.

"I haven't had these in a while," she said. "Now all I need is a cup of hot chocolate."

"They're selling some right over there," Declan replied. "We'll make that our next stop."

They sat down on a bench with Rae between them to finish eating.

Everleigh admired the red and while poinsettias in green pots that sat on the porch of the house on the corner.

An hour passed as they walked up and down the main street. Rae was so happy to be out of the house that she hopped, skipped and did a little dance.

"She's a ball of energy," Declan said.

"Yes, she is," Everleigh responded.

Rae wasn't a fan of the roasted chestnuts, so she stopped at the vendor selling gingerbread cookies.

They headed home shortly after that. Declan didn't want to keep them away from the house for too long.

After Rae went up to bed, Everleigh and Declan settled at the dining room table to discuss Powell's victims. It was becoming a routine, and though it was for a grim reason, she found she was starting to look forward to this part of her day.

She opened her padfolio and picked up her pen. "Where do we start?"

"It's an official investigation now."

She sighed. She'd known it was coming. "Okay, but I can't just sit here and do nothing. I've helped law enforcement in the past, consulting on several cases in Savannah. This concerns my daughter's safety. I can help."

"This goes against my better judgment, Everleigh."

"Don't make me beg."

After a moment, he said, "Lena Jones... I was finally able to locate her. She'd changed her name to Michelle. Unfortunately, she passed away a month ago. She had cancer."

"I'm sorry to hear that."

"I spoke with her husband," Declan stated. "According to him, she never wanted to talk about her past. He said that she was seeing a therapist until she got really sick. He didn't know anything about what had happened to her."

"Now what?"

"Let's look at the victims who had children at the time of their deaths," Declan suggested.

Everleigh checked her notes. "I think I've narrowed it down to eight...no, seven victims who had children."

Declan eyed her in surprise.

"I told you I could be useful," she said, grinning. "We already knew about the children of the first victim. You ruled them out."

"Yeah, we can move from the two surviving children."

Declan and Everleigh discussed what he'd found on two of the seven victims left on the list.

"Marcia Ricks had a daughter," he said while going through notes on his iPad. "That daughter is currently working as a guidance counselor at a high school in Loma Linda, California. She's married with three children."

She made notes, then looked back up at him to continue.

"Samara James was the mother of four," Declan stated. "One son is in prison. A daughter is a bible-study teacher—she's married to a pastor."

"And the other two?"

"Another daughter manages a fast-food restaurant. I haven't found anything on the last daughter as of yet. The next victim is Luanne Shelby."

"Do you know anything about her?"

"No. I'll run a check on her the first thing tomorrow. The same with the other three victims on our list."

"If this doesn't pan out, what do we do next?" Everleigh asked.

"I could go see Powell…"

"Why would you do that?" she blurted. "If you do that, Declan…you risk exposing me and Rae. That's the last thing I need to deal with—my serial-killer daddy. I don't want anything to do with that man."

"I don't have to mention you at all."

"You don't think he'd wonder why you're suddenly so interested in him?"

"I could just tell him that I study criminals, or that I'm looking into the deaths of his relatives, Everleigh."

"I'd rather you didn't talk to him at all," she said.

"Okay," Declan responded. "I won't."

"Unless it's *absolutely* necessary," Everleigh amended. "I want to find this person as much as you do. I just don't want more trouble in the process."

Declan drove around the block and parked a few houses away from Everleigh's home. He settled back in his seat, making himself comfortable.

His phone rang.

"Everything okay?" he asked.

Everleigh's voice came through the speaker. "You need to go home."

He laughed. "How did you know?"

"I'm learning how your mind works. We're fine, Declan," she said. "You don't have to sit in that car half the night. It's cold out there and besides, the police still drive by often."

"Then I'll leave after I speak to the officer on duty."

"Okay…thanks. Rae and I appreciate you."

They talked a few minutes more before hanging up.

A police cruiser rolled past the house.

Declan was about to leave when a dark sedan turned on her street. It drove slowly, and when it didn't stop, he breathed a sigh of relief. He watched until it turned the corner.

He was about to leave when the motion lights in Everleigh's backyard suddenly came on, lighting up that area. Declan jumped out of his car and took off running toward her house.

His hand on his holster, he crept around to the backyard.

"Declan, he's gone," Everleigh said from her patio. "When the lights came on, he ran off. I saw him from the window." She had a bat in her hand. "It was Wyle. I got a clear look at his face."

"What was he wearing?"

"A hoodie, a jacket—everything dark."

He glanced around. "No cameras back here?"

"I thought the motion detectors would be enough, but I'll be adding one first thing tomorrow." Shivering, Everleigh gestured to the door. "It's cold. Let's go inside. I'm sure Wyle's long gone by now."

They sat down in the family room.

"I guess it's a good thing you were still on the island after all," she said.

"What were you going to do with that?" he asked, pointing to the bat.

"Beat Wyle to a pulp, then use my Taser on him."

Declan bit back his laughter. "Okay."

"I was on the baseball team from middle school to college," Everleigh stated. "Trust me, I know how to swing a bat."

"And the Taser? Have you ever used one?"

"No, but I know how. I've taken several self-defense

classes." She got up and looked out the window. "I'm also a black belt in karate. I can defend myself."

She certainly could.

Turning to face him, she said, "Now we know that Wyle is here and he's after me."

Declan nodded in agreement.

"So what do we do now?"

"I'll try to get you and Rae into a safe house. If you don't mind, I'll stay here tonight."

Her arms folded across her chest, Everleigh nodded. "That's perfectly fine. I'll feel better with you being here, honestly. You can stay in the guest room down here. I'll see you in the morning."

"You okay?"

"I feel better knowing that I wasn't imagining Wyle being on campus that day."

Declan eyed her. "Did he see you?"

"He did," she responded. "He seemed startled. For a second, I thought Wyle was going to say something to me. He just took off running instead."

"Doesn't sound like he has the heart of a killer."

"No, it doesn't," Everleigh said.

An hour later, Everleigh was still awake, so she went downstairs to the kitchen.

She sliced several oranges into wedges, putting them into plastic snack bags. Next, she chopped up an onion and green and red bell peppers, placing each of them in separate containers.

When Declan entered the kitchen, she said, "I'm sorry if I woke you. I was trying not to make much noise."

"You didn't wake me." Pointing to the oranges, he commented, "Looks like you had some trouble going back to sleep, though."

"Whenever I can't sleep, I meal-prep. It relaxes me." She pointed to the teapot on the stove. "Would you like some tea? The water's already hot."

"Sure."

"Lemon and ginger, okay?"

"Yeah," Declan replied.

They made small talk while they sat at the breakfast table drinking their tea.

"This isn't how I envisioned Rae and I would be spending the holidays," Everleigh sighed. "I never thought we'd be running for our lives."

"I have an BOLO out on Wyle. He is to be taken to the precinct and I plan on interviewing him myself."

She took a sip of her tea. "I wish I could be there."

"I'll let you know what happens," Declan said. "I still don't think that he's our killer, but I'm hoping he can lead us to the perp."

"If these are two separate threats, then we'll be fighting blind." She shuddered at the thought.

When they finished, she bade him good-night, then went up to her bedroom.

Rae was still sleeping soundly, without fear.

Although Everleigh had been trained in self-defense, she considered retrieving her mother's gun for protection but really didn't want one in the house with Rae. To ease her mind and the quakes in her serenity, she reread Psalm 91. It always gave her comfort and was a gentle reminder that God was the best security system in the world.

"Hey, why don't you and Rae come stay at my place for a few days?" Declan suggested the next morning. "It'll do you both some good to get away from the house. I have plenty of space and you won't have to worry about looking over your shoulder while you're there. Besides, I make an amazing chili. I top it with sour cream and green onions."

"We love chili," she responded. "How do you serve yours? With corn chips or corn bread? You can't go wrong either way."

"Corn bread."

"Sounds great," Everleigh murmured.

"So what do you say?"

"Sure. I think it'll do us both good to get out of here for a day or so."

"It's perfect," Declan responded. He was going to enjoy entertaining them at his home. He would also rest better knowing they were safe and under his protection.

Everleigh headed to the staircase. "I'll pack really quick."

"Are we going somewhere?" Rae asked when she reached the second level.

"Little girls shouldn't listen to adult conversations."

"Are we?"

"Yes. We're going to stay with Mr. Declan for a couple of days."

"Yay!" Rae broke out into a little dance.

Everleigh couldn't help but chuckle. "Really? It's like that."

"Mama, we hardly ever go anywhere."

Rae was right. Even before this threat, they hadn't gone out much since moving to the island—the only time they really went anywhere was for work and school. Her daughter was lonely. And if she was honest, she'd admit that she was, too.

This would be good for them both.

"Come help me pack," Everleigh said.

Thirty minutes later, they were on their way.

When they turned into Declan's neighborhood twenty

minutes later, she was a bit surprised that he didn't live in a condo or a town house. The brick home was a fairly large one, with three garages, and looked to be about three thousand square feet.

"Your house is pretty," Rae said.

Everleigh agreed.

"Thank you," he responded. "I've been in this house for two years now."

"It looks new. Did you have it built?"

"Yeah. I prefer custom-built homes."

That was a dream Everleigh had had at one point in her life. It was a dream she shared with Britt—a dream long gone.

NINE

"Doggy," Rae gasped when they walked into Declan's house. She rushed to Everleigh's side and cowered. "Is he gonna bite me?"

"No, she's very friendly. You don't have to be afraid of her."

Peeking from behind her mother, Rae asked, "What's her name?"

"Billie," Declan responded. "Here, if you kneel down like this and hold your hand out, she'll come over and sniff you. That's how she says hello."

Rae came out from behind Everleigh and did as instructed. Sure enough, the Labrador retriever came up to her gently. As the dog sniffed her fingers, Everleigh ran her palm over Billie's glossy coat.

"She's beautiful," Everleigh murmured. She loved dogs but her late husband was allergic, so they'd never had one.

A few licks from Billie and Rae had changed her mind in favor of dogs, too. "You're a good doggy," she said. "So cute... I like you, Billie. You can be my friend."

Declan grabbed the suitcases out of his SUV and started back toward the house. Everleigh grabbed her leather tote and fell in beside him. Declan showed her to a bedroom upstairs with a small sitting area off to one side and a private bath.

"This is where you and Rae will be sleeping," he said.

A beautiful coverlet in teal and navy covered a king-size bed with a padded headboard.

Everleigh turned to him. "Is this your room?"

"No, my room is downstairs."

She relaxed. "Oh, good. I didn't want to put you out."

"Well, I'll leave you to it," Declan stated. "I'll head down to the kitchen to find something for us to eat."

The door closed, shutting out his tall frame.

"This room is so pretty," Rae said, sinking down on the bed.

"Yes, it is."

"We're gonna have so much fun here."

Everleigh smiled. "Starting right now…"

She glanced down at her wedding rings. After her husband's death, she had thrown herself into her work, her daughter and taking care of her mother, but it never occurred to Everleigh that she hadn't really moved on.

Until now.

She told herself that she didn't want to rush through her grief. That she had to make sure her daughter was okay. Everleigh didn't want to neglect Rae. She vowed to be there for her as much as was necessary. It wouldn't cushion the blow of her daughter's loss, but it would help her heal.

Everleigh remembered experiencing a wave of apprehension when her husband left for work that day. It was as if she knew deep down that something bad was going to happen. She'd spent most of the day in prayer, asking God to protect her husband; to bring him home safe.

That evening, there had been a knock on the door.

She knew before Britt's supervisor and a union official spoke a word. Her husband had died in the line of duty.

Everleigh felt in that moment that God hadn't heard her fervent prayers, or worse… He had chosen to ignore them. She remembered telling her mother that God had taken her husband from her.

Deloris had placed a gentle hand on Everleigh's shoulder and said, "I want you to try a different perspective. Consider that God welcomed Britt home."

It helped to look at his leaving through that lens, but it didn't stop her from missing him, or the heartache that his dying left behind.

After setting up a movie for Rae to watch, Declan said, "We can talk in my office."

Everleigh followed him down the hall into what looked like a library.

"You love books, I see," she observed. "From the looks of it, you're a mystery buff. You also like the classics and historical fiction, too."

"I checked out your books, too," he responded. "You like psychological thrillers and mysteries, romance and I glimpsed a few historical-fiction titles."

"We have that in common." She smiled when she glimpsed the framed degrees on the wall along with a beautiful display of abstract artwork. A jar filled with pencils, pens and highlighters sat to the left of the computer monitor. To the right was another jar filled with thumb drives. Everleigh noticed several colorful Post-it notes tacked to his monitor.

"Where you able to get any new information?" she asked, sitting down in the chair facing his desk.

"Not yet. I did request Olivia Ragland's file. She was Powell's last known victim. I'll let you know what I find out."

"Thank you. I just wish we could put a name and a face to whoever wrote that letter, if we're assuming it wasn't Wyle. It's not easy fighting the invisible man."

"He won't be able to remain invisible," Declan said. "Eventually, he's got to show himself."

He had grown tired of waiting around for orders. He waited until it was the black of night before making his move; the darkness was his protection. He'd convinced their *friend* to help him hack into her home security account and disable the alarm system. This time there wasn't anything standing between him and the entrance to Everleigh Taylor's house.

Her house had large arched windows in the front. He imagined that light from all four seasons poured through, gracing the air and illuminating the gray-stained wooden floor. The walls were light. It was too dark to see the true color, but even with the moonlight creeping through the windows, he saw that the baseboards were bold white.

The banister was made of oak, its grain flowing as water might, in waves of comforting brown hues. The living room was to the left. His eyes traveled over his surroundings. Nice, neat...everything in its place. It appeared to be a medley of memories, of photographs adorning the walls, all of them conjuring emotions of sweet moments— something he knew nothing about.

He and his brother had never grown up in a place like this, even when their mother was alive. But she kept their tiny apartment clean and neat. Their father cared more about getting high than he did a suitable place to raise a family. It was the reason why their mother left. She was determined to raise her boys by herself.

They'd been excited about the new apartment. She could only afford a one-bedroom, so she'd invested in a used sofa bed. Whenever they were home with her, she'd let him and his brother sleep in the bedroom while she took the sofa bed.

His mother was a good woman and she didn't deserve to die so young. She didn't deserve to be murdered.

Upon these walls were the pictures of the daughter, so obviously loved. His eyes traveled back to a photograph of Everleigh.

I want to hear her scream.

He silently made his way to the staircase, then growled when he found the bedrooms upstairs empty.

They were gone.

"You can't hide from me," he yelled. "I'll find you."

In his fury, he snatched a photo of Everleigh and her daughter off the wall and tossed it to the floor.

TEN

Declan's wooded backyard was a sanctuary for nature and his place of serenity. It was fenced-in and private; safe and secure. Rae had spent the past hour outside with Billie, running back and forth. It thrilled Everleigh to see her little girl laughing without a care in the world. She wanted to keep it that way.

"She's having a ball," she said, watching from within the screened-in porch, Declan by her side.

"So is Billie," he responded. "She loves children."

"Obviously, you do, too."

"Guilty," Declan said with a tiny smile.

She sat down in one of the chairs. "This is just what we needed."

He sat down in the other chair. "Anytime you need to get away, you're welcome to come here."

"I can't get over how generous you are—first your time and now your home."

"I want to be a good friend," he told her. "I tend to treat people the way I'd want to be treated—it's what my parents taught me."

"They should be extremely proud of you, Declan."

"You certainly know how to make a man feel real proud, Everleigh."

"I'm only speaking the truth."

"What do you think about tacos for dinner tomorrow night?" he asked.

"Sounds great. Rae will love it. She's a huge fan of tacos."

He leaned toward her and whispered, "So am I. Beef, chicken, shrimp taco—love them all. It will be a create-your-own-taco night."

"Yum," Everleigh murmured. "Although it won't be taco Tuesday."

He chuckled. "No, it won't. We make our own rules in this house."

"Hey, I like the idea of taco Wednesdays."

"I ordered some stuff from the grocery store," Declan said as he stood up. "It should be here soon."

"Rae, it's time to come inside," Everleigh told her.

"Five more minutes, please."

"Okay, but that's it. I want you to clean up for lunch."

"Rae, how would you like to help me cook the meat for dinner tomorrow?" Declan asked. "We're having tacos."

"Yay," she squealed. "Mama likes shrimp on hers. I like beef and chicken."

Rae ran toward the porch with Billie on her heels. She stood there for a moment to catch her breath.

"Let's get you into a nice warm bath," Everleigh said.

"I have a virtual meeting with a student," Declan announced. "I'll be in my office if you need me."

Half an hour later, she was in the kitchen when he walked in with the groceries.

Everleigh pointed to the frying pan. "I was about to make some grilled-cheese sandwiches and tomato soup. Would you like some?"

Declan grinned. "You're taking me back to my college days. Those late-night grilled-cheese sandwiches used to get me through a lot of study sessions. I don't think I've had one since I left school."

She stood with her back at the counter while he put away packages of beef, shrimp, chicken breasts, cheese and other items inside the refrigerator.

"Really?"

"It's true."

"I'll have to change that right now," she said.

I can really get used to this.

Declan gave himself a mental shake. He couldn't afford to live in a fantasy world. He needed to stay focused on the reality of this situation.

After they finished eating, he decided to put some distance between himself and Everleigh.

"I'll be in my room working until it's time to cook dinner," Declan announced. "Do you need anything before I disappear?"

"No, we're good. I'll do my best to keep Rae from disturbing you."

"Let her enjoy herself." Declan wanted to say more, but thought better of it. "I'll see you in a few hours."

"Okay."

He walked away swiftly before his prized control faded and he kissed her. Everleigh trusted him and he didn't want to tamper with that trust. This was a safe space for her and Rae. He would never violate that.

Everleigh and Rae were in danger. His job was to protect them, keep them safe. Not pretend like they were a happy little family. Once they neutralized the threat, things between him and Everleigh would go back to the way they were before.

Well, maybe not exactly, he amended. They knew each other better now; perhaps they had laid the foundation of friendship. But that was about it. Declan shouldn't expect anything more to happen between them.

Declan sat down at the small desk in his bedroom. There were times when it was late at night or he just didn't feel like going to his home office, so he would work here instead. However, neither his mind nor his heart was focused on anything other than Everleigh. Already he missed the sound of her voice.

His pride would not let him venture back to the main level—it was too soon. He'd told Everleigh that he would be working most of the afternoon. He had to keep up the facade.

In that moment, Declan wished things could be different.

After spending the morning with Rae outside, they sat down to go through their notes while she was napping.

"You may have told me this already, but I don't recall," Declan said. "Where did your mom live when she was attacked by Powell?"

"She lived a block away from the college she attended."

"How was she able to get away?"

"My grandfather had given her a gun to protect herself. She was able to get off a shot, but I don't think she hit him. It scared him off, though."

"Someone would've heard the shot that night," he responded. "They might have called the police. Maybe they saw or heard something that night."

"You're right."

"If we go back to the estimated time of your conception, I might be able to isolate a time frame and we can check to see if someone reported shots fired."

Her eyes widened. "Do you really think we can do that, Declan?"

"We're certainly going to try."

"This other woman… Olivia Ragland," Everleigh said. "I saw that she lived in Atlanta at the time of her murder. Do you have her address?"

"I do," he responded.

She performed an online search. "Looks like she lived a block away from the college my mother attended. I wish I could remember my mom's old address. A cousin and I visited that area once. I bet Powell was hanging around the school and followed women home."

Declan nodded in agreement.

"It's entirely possible that he tried to talk to her and my mom rebuffed him," Everleigh said. "Her rejection would've set him off. He probably did the same thing with Olivia. I'm sure he was stalking them."

"I found out right before I came down that one of the women who survived, Kathy Kitt, was murdered a week before Powell was arrested," Declan said. "She was killed six months after he raped her. Another man is suspected of killing her."

"We know that Lena died recently, but is the other survivor still alive?" Everleigh asked.

He shook his head. "Not sure. Sarah Mason disappeared. Some believe she went into hiding, but her parents insist it was foul play. They say she wouldn't have left without a word to them. She's listed as missing. This was during the time Powell was roaming around free."

"Declan, do you think Powell returned to finish what he started?" she asked.

"I'm going to discuss these findings with my superiors. I'd like to read the investigation reports."

"Was the suspect ever arrested for Kathy's murder?"

He shook his head. "Her case is still open. But forensic evidence suggested Powell wasn't at the scene."

"A man like Powell…he'd want to silence the women," Everleigh mused. "He didn't like losing, so he'd never give up until he did just that. Silence them." She couldn't help but wonder if Powell had looked for her mother. If so, it must have frustrated him to find her gone. Suddenly, it dawned on Everleigh that her mother had also lived on Beech, the same street as Oliva Ragland.

The thought stayed with her all through the evening as she showered and prepared for bed. She decided to talk to Declan about it.

After checking on Rae, Everleigh brushed out her hair, and pulled on a soft fleece sweatsuit and wool socks. She headed down the hall to his office. There was no light beneath the door. He had probably gone to bed. She thought of the way her gaze kept drifting over his wide shoulders, muscular frame and long legs during the preparation of dinner. *Maybe I'd better not bother him. This can wait until morning.*

But, no, this was important. Renewing her resolve, Everleigh went downstairs and knocked on Declan's bedroom door. He abruptly pulled it open, causing her to stumble forward into his arms.

"Everleigh…" he said, helping her regain her balance. "Did you need something?"

"I've been thinking about that address in Atlanta where Olivia Ragland lived—I'd like to see how close it was to my mother's old apartment. She lived a block away from the college. When I saw that address, it nagged at me because I knew I'd heard of the street before. I'm pretty sure that she and my mom lived on the same street."

They went down the hall to his office.

"These are the only apartments on that street within five blocks of the college," Declan said.

"Then they must have lived in the same complex," she

murmured. Everleigh looked up at him. "He attacked two women in the same area. I guess when my mom didn't report the attack, it bolstered his confidence."

"I agree," Declan said, "because that's the only time he ever struck twice in the same city."

Declan had felt a nearly magnetic charge in the air when he opened his bedroom door to find Everleigh standing there. His gaze had locked on hers and when she'd smiled, everything inside him tightened. It was getting harder and harder to keep his emotions under control.

When he left his bedroom shortly after seven, he was surprised to find Everleigh already up and in the kitchen. "I thought maybe you'd sleep in this morning," he said. "We were up until two thirty."

"Cooking calms me down," she responded. "I hope you don't mind that I took over your kitchen."

"I don't mind at all." He retrieved a mug from the cabinet and set it down on the counter. "I need a cup of coffee." Declan eyed the square baking pan covered with foil sitting on top of the stove. "What's that?"

"Biscuits. My mother's recipe. There's also bacon."

"I could sure use a couple slices."

"I can make scrambled eggs if you want."

"Biscuits and bacon will do."

Everleigh poured some freshly brewed coffee into his mug, which Declan carried over to the table. She took him some biscuits, butter and strawberry jam. She filled her own plate and mug, and then joined him at the table.

"I thought about what you said last night. I'm going to look deeper into Kathy Kitt's death." He took a sip from his mug.

"Good, because I really think Powell was responsible," Everleigh said. She cradled her mug between her palms, letting the heat seep into her skin. "Kathy could identify him, so he possibly shut her up permanently. The main reason my mom and Lena survived is most likely because they left town right after the attacks."

"You're probably right," he said. "Powell couldn't find them."

Declan took a sip of coffee. "I got Olivia Ragland's file and went through it from cover to cover. Her ex-husband and two young sons found her body."

She looked up at him. "Oh, how horrible for them. Very traumatic."

"Everleigh, do you have any of your mother's personal files?"

"Yes, I put all that stuff in a storage facility on the island. Why?"

"We need to go there—I want to check on something."

"What's on your mind?" she asked.

"Let's consider your theory on Kathy Kitt. Powell hunted her down and killed her. He doesn't like to lose."

"What are you getting at?" she asked.

"The apartments where Olivia Ragland lived—the ones we think your mom lived in, too."

"Yes?"

"What if they lived in the very same apartment? Olivia might have moved in after your mother fled."

"You think that Powell went back to finish what he started with my mother but found Olivia instead," Everleigh said. "If that's true…his rage would've escalated when he discovered that my mom escaped him a second time."

"That could be the reason why Olivia's death was more brutal than the others," Declan replied.

"If this is true, then…her sons—maybe it's one of them."

"It's certainly a possibility. I have my mother's possessions in storage. Maybe there's something there that can help us."

"It won't hurt to check it out."

Later, at the storage facility, they went through several boxes while Rae sat quietly in a corner with her tablet. She was sullen because Billie couldn't come with them.

After the third box turned up nothing, Everleigh said, "My mom kept practically everything, but I'm not sure she would've kept anything from her time in Atlanta."

"If we don't find anything here, we can always go to Atlanta and talk to the apartment manager," he suggested.

"Actually, I think we should do that," Everleigh responded. "We'd probably be more successful."

"Are you serious?"

"Yes, I am," she said. "We should go to Atlanta."

"We can leave first thing tomorrow morning."

After they left the storage unit, Declan said. "Why don't I drop y'all back at the house now to pack whatever you need? I need to run to the precinct, anyway, to talk to my supervisor. I shouldn't be gone too long. A couple of hours at the most. I really think I have something solid to present now."

"We've got everything we need with us. We can stay put while you go to the precinct," she assured him.

"Stay inside while I'm gone," he said, after letting them inside his house.

"That won't be a problem. I'll get dinner started."

"My kitchen is all yours," he responded with a smile, and headed out the door.

A few hours later, Everleigh was nowhere in sight, but the scent of seasoned beef waited for Declan when he got home. On the stovetop was a pan of taco shells.

He smiled. So this is what it felt like to come home to a family.

The feelings Everleigh evoked in him weren't easy to explain or articulate. Even when she wasn't around, his heart ached in his chest and Declan found himself hungering for her presence in his life. Whenever they weren't together, he felt a certain warmth as the prolonged anticipation of seeing Everleigh almost seemed unbearable.

She strolled into the kitchen, surprising him. "Everything's ready for taco Wednesday."

"A man can get used to all of this really easy."

Everleigh smiled. "Enjoy it while you can."

ELEVEN

Everleigh took a deep breath. She was in way over her head with Declan Blanchet. She liked him way more than she could ever have anticipated. But then, she never thought that they would be spending so much time together.

Their Christmas break had started with her and Rae staying with him, and now they were on their way to Atlanta.

"Are we gonna have Christmas in Atlanta?" her daughter asked.

"No, sweetie. It's just a short visit. We might stop in to see some family. Cousin Bonnie lives there."

"Yay. I love her. She's so fun."

Everleigh chuckled and said to Declan, "My cousin is a big kid at heart. Whenever she came to visit, Bonnie would play with dolls, color—whatever Rae wanted to do. I'm going to give her a call to see if Rae can spend some time with her."

He nodded in understanding.

She and Declan could move about freely if Rae wasn't with them. Everleigh wanted to keep her daughter in the dark about everything that was going on around her, sparing her the trauma that came with victimization.

Everleigh thought of the trauma Olivia Ragland's sons must have endured when they found their mother's battered and mutilated body. She wouldn't be surprised if one or both of them were now focused on getting some type of justice. They had no evidence to support this theory, but her instincts told her they were getting closer to the truth.

They had just gotten back to their hotel from dinner. They had arrived in Atlanta before noon. Rae sat on the floor beside Billie, talking to her and rubbing her fur. One of her favorite movies was on the television.

Everleigh pulled a pack of playing cards out of her tote. "Do you remember how badly I beat you in Spades the other night?"

"You beat *me*?" Laughing, Declan shook his head. "I don't think so. I have no memory of anything like that."

She grinned. "Well, why don't we play a quick game right now."

"I don't think you want to do that, Everleigh."

"Yes, I do," she responded while shuffling the deck of cards and placing them face down on the table.

Everleigh sank down to the floor.

Declan followed suit.

He drew the first card. "I have a ten."

Everleigh drew next. "You go first. I have a four."

She laughed at the expression on his face when he drew the next card. "What's wrong?"

"I'm fine. I got this."

She won the first round.

"Oaky. Okay," Declan said. "I'll give you that win."

"You're not giving me anything," she responded with a laugh. "I won that round on my own merit."

"Learning something new about you. You're very competitive." Declan hadn't had this much fun in a long time. He felt an eager affection coming from Everleigh. Every time her gaze met his, Declan felt his heart turn over in response.

"It's your turn," Everleigh said, bringing him out of his reverie.

He won the second round. "Okay, let's play one more game to decide the winner."

Everleigh nodded in agreement.

It was hard to keep his attention on the game. He was physically attracted to Everleigh, but he was also attracted to her mind.

"I guess you're the winner," Declan said a short while later.

He checked his watch, and then said, "I should probably go to my room. Rae looks like she's tired and sleepy."

He rose to his feet and then assisted Everleigh up.

They stood facing one another.

He hesitated a moment before walking to the door. Declan turned around to face Everleigh.

"Declan…"

He tingled as she said his name. He would've preferred to sweep her into his arms and hold her close to him for a long time. He wanted to kiss her.

His gaze traveled to her left hand.

"I'd better go," he whispered.

"I'll call you after Rae goes to sleep," she said.

"Talk to you then."

"Keep your head in the game," he whispered as he walked the short distance to the room next door.

Stunned, Everleigh sat down on the edge of the bed. She couldn't get past the look Declan had given her, or the way he'd stared at her lips. It was almost as if he wanted to kiss her.

She shook away the thought.

I'm misreading his intentions.

At least this was what she was telling herself. Everleigh wouldn't allow herself to believe that there was anything igniting between them.

Declan saw her as a woman in jeopardy. A woman he'd agreed to protect.

But what if she was right about what she saw in his expression. She hadn't imagined the warmth she'd glimpsed in the depths of his eyes.

Even so, he was too much of a gentleman to cross boundaries; Everleigh knew this much about him.

The deeper question was how she felt about all this. She wasn't sure.

Everleigh chocked it up to her emotions being all over the place due to the current stressors in her life, mixed with her grief. She was feeling a bit overwhelmed and unsettled, although she didn't want to show it. She was taking it day-by-day in an effort to keep calm so as not to upset Rae.

The little girl had no idea that her life was in danger.

She glanced over at her sleeping child, then joined her in the king-size bed.

Everleigh didn't fall asleep right away.

She lay there, staring up at the ceiling and wondering if she'd ever be able to feel safe again. Or if she could ever open her heart to someone new.

The next day, Declan and Everleigh headed out to drop Rae off with her cousin Bonnie.

He was still waiting to hear back from the apartment manager.

"What does your cousin do?" Declan asked as he followed his GPS to Bonnie's house.

"She's a nurse. She worked a double shift yesterday and

didn't get off until seven this morning. She said she got a couple hours' sleep and is excited to spend time with Rae."

"How long has she lived in Atlanta?"

"All of her life, as far as I know," Everleigh responded as she stared out the passenger window.

"Was she close to your mom?" he asked.

"Her mom and my mom were close," she answered. "And Bonnie and I were close. Her mom died two years before mine."

"Is there anyone else you can think of in Atlanta who could shed some light on your mother's time here?"

"Nobody that I know," Everleigh stated. "Most of her family lived in the Savannah-Hinesville area. After what happened, my mom never wanted to come back here. Now I fully understand why. Atlanta held terrible memories for her."

Ten minutes later, they were on Bonnie's doorstep.

"Oh, my *goodness*! Look at my little Rae of sunshine," Bonnie gushed. "You've grown into a ball of more cuteness."

Ray broke into a big grin. "Hey, cousin Bonnie."

Everleigh introduced Declan.

"Very nice to meet you." He could see a family resemblance between the two women. The high cheekbones, the same complexion and warm brown eyes.

His phone rang.

"I need to take this," he said. "I'll wait for you outside."

Declan hoped to have some good news for Everleigh. He'd called the manager's office this morning and left a message.

They were just now returning the call and he hoped it was good news.

"Girl, that's one fine piece of chocolate," Bonnie whispered. "Are you sure y'all just friends?"

"I can't believe you just said that," she responded with a chuckle.

"He's gorgeous."

"Enough about Declan," Everleigh said. "Are you sure you're up to Rae spending the night with you?"

"Of course, I am," Bonnie replied. "We're going to have a good time together. You and Declan take care of your business."

She hugged her cousin. "Thank you."

When they drove away her cousin's house, Everleigh said, "I already miss my baby."

"Are you sure you want to leave Rae there?"

"I know she's safe with Bonnie. We just haven't ever been apart. I told her to call me if Rae wants us to pick her up."

"Will you be upset if she doesn't?" Declan asked.

"I don't think so… I don't know." She glanced over at him. "I think I might."

"What do you tell your clients? Baby steps, right?"

Everleigh nodded. "Yes."

"We can always pick her up if it's necessary. And Bonnie doesn't live that far from the hotel."

"This is true… Okay, I'm focused now."

"Good. That was the current manager who called when we were at your cousin's house. She has only been with the company five years," Declan said. "Ezra Stone was the manager back when your mom lived there. He quit after Oliva Ragland died. Apparently, they have some new software they're using now. She said the old rental records were archived in a storage facility."

"Are we going to try to find this Ezra Stone?" she asked.

"Yeah. It shouldn't be too hard. We can see if he's on any social media."

They decided to have lunch at a local Italian restaurant.

On the way to their table, Declan told her a joke, he'd heard from one of his coworkers.

"You have an incredible sense of humor," Everleigh commented as she scanned her menu. She took a sip of her ice water. "I really like getting to know this side of you."

He laughed. "I'm assuming you originally thought I was pretty boring."

"Not really," she replied. "Well… I didn't really know what to think about you. You just seemed so serious all the time."

"You're not the first person to say that about me."

She met his gaze. "I hope that I didn't make you feel bad."

"You didn't." Declan reached across the table to hold her hand. "It's good to hear how you come across from other people."

He picked up his menu and began looking it over. "I think I'm having the chicken marsala," he said. "Do you know what you want?"

"I'm in the mood for fettuccine Alfredo with mush-rooms."

They gave the server their orders when he returned to the table.

"Wyle Gaines is in the wind," Declan announced. "He may have already left Charleston."

"I can believe that," she responded. "He seemed so slip-pery to me when he was ingratiating himself to my mother. It doesn't surprise me that he'd be a coward now."

The waiter returned with their meals.

Declan blessed the food.

Everleigh sampled her fettuccine Alfredo. "This is de-licious."

"Mine is really good, too," he responded.

Everleigh's eyes traveled the dining area. "It feels great

being out like this among people again. It's nice not having to worry about someone trying to do me harm."

Declan wiped his mouth on the edge of his napkin. "I think we're getting close to finding out who's after you. Hopefully, Ezra Stone will be able to give us more information about the Ragland family. He probably won't be able to tell us much about the boys, Neil and Ellis—they were really young."

"You seem pretty positive that the person after me could be one or both of her sons without any real proof."

"I've never been one to believe in coincidences. It's been way too many since you got that letter, Everleigh."

"Oh, I agree. Too many."

"I'm not saying it's definitely them, but this gives us a place to start."

They left the restaurant and returned to the hotel.

Seated in Everleigh's room, they reviewed everything they'd learned about Olivia Ragland's death.

"Whatever happened to Olivia's husband?" she asked.

"I looked Ellison Ragland up. There isn't a current driving record, nothing about employment—he seemed to have just disappeared. Not even a death certificate."

"That's interesting…"

He nodded in agreement. "He's on my list of potential suspects, too. I want to be as sure as I can be about this," Declan said. "Now that we have his address, I'm hoping what we learn from Ezra Stone will give me some additional information that will connect all the pieces of this puzzle."

TWELVE

"I guess you still ain't talkin' to me," he said.

"Wh-Why should I bother? It's not like you ever l-listen to me," his brother responded. "I t-told you not to go to her house. Not only did you go there, you broke in."

"Nothin' happened. I disabled her alarm. Besides she and the little girl weren't even home."

"Man, your rage is gonna end up gettin' you l-locked up."

"As long as she's dead… I don't care. Besides, you the one who told me I should hate Powell and his entire family. You told me that they have a sickness runnin' in that bloodline."

His brother uttered, "I hate being back in Georgia. I hate this p-place with a passion."

"We're staying in Temple for the night."

"I thought we was going to Villa Rica," his brother said, confusion coloring his tone.

"We are," he responded. "We just not staying there. That town too small. Everybody knows everybody. I want to take care of business and get out."

"Man…" his brother said. "You know who you sound like right now… you need to chill."

"I'll chill when I'm dead."

* * *

Spending time with mother and child made Declan yearn for something he never really thought he'd have—a family. Past relationships had been ruined because of his chosen profession. Former girlfriends said they could handle his being in law enforcement, but in the end…they couldn't. The divorce rate was high in his field. He saw it happen within his own family. His sister's marriage ended because of her job with Homeland Security.

Declan was struggling to maintain control over his emotions and stay professional, but what he felt for Everleigh could no longer be denied. However, now wasn't the time to act on those feelings. He also knew as long as she wore her wedding rings, she wasn't ready to move forward in a relationship.

He strode out of his hotel room with purpose. It was time to meet Everleigh for breakfast.

She opened her door just as he walked up.

"Prompt as always," she said with a smile. "I like that about you."

"It's a quality I greatly appreciate as well."

They took the elevator downstairs.

"I called Rae. She told me she was having the best time with Bonnie. She asked if she could spend another night with her. I think I'm jealous."

"Your daughter adores you," Declan said.

"I know. I just miss my baby."

"So what did you tell her?"

"I told her that she could stay another night. She sounded so happy."

"I'll do my best to keep you entertained."

Everleigh eyed him. "I'm going to hold you to that."

After they'd shared breakfast at the hotel restaurant,

they headed out to find Ezra Stone. Declan had secured his address the night before.

They walked up concrete steps to the raggedy wooden porch and knocked on the front door.

"What you want?" a man yelled from inside. "We ain't buying nothing."

"We're here to talk to Ezra Stone."

"What you want with my pops?" The door swung open wide, revealing a middle-aged man with a heavy scowl.

"We'd like to speak with him about an incident that happened when he managed the Catalina Apartments," Declan said.

"That ain't gonna happen, sir. My pops died seven months ago. He was murdered and the police ain't did nothing to find the person responsible."

"I'm very sorry for your loss," Everleigh stated. "I lost my mother six months ago. She used to live in the apartments during the time your father was the manager."

He eyed her. "How did she die? Your mama."

"She had cancer."

"What was her name?"

"Deloris Sanderson."

"*Wait a minute*... I remember her," he said, and his expression became animated. "She'd babysit me sometimes when she didn't have class. Deloris sure was a nice lady. I remember she was gonna be a doctor. She studied a lot."

Everleigh smiled. "That's right. She ended up being a nurse. Mama decided not to go to medical school."

He held the door open and stepped aside to let them enter.

"Sorry about earlier. I'm Jeremiah Stone."

Once they were seated in the living room, he said, "I used to ask my dad about Deloris and why she moved away. He always said that it was probably best that she did. I didn't have a clue what that meant. Not back then."

"What do you mean?" Everleigh asked.

"I found out later that your mama was attacked and that's why she left the apartment without telling anyone. Then when that other lady moved into that same apartment and was murdered. Well, my dad…it did him in— he couldn't stay there after that. He was never the same. It ate at him all these years, so the police said his death was a suicide. But it wasn't. He would never kill himself. That wasn't him at all."

"Wait…" Everleigh said. "Are you talking about Olivia Ragland?"

"Yep, she be the one."

She frowned and said to Declan, "My mom must have told Ezra about what happened to her."

Jeremiah shook his head. "It was her daddy—your granddaddy—that told my pops. The way my pops told it, he came by maybe a week after she took off. Packed up her apartment. He let slip that something bad had happened to your mama. My pops, he felt horrible when he heard that she'd been attacked. If he'd known… I know that he would've tried to help your mama."

"Did my grandfather say anything more?"

"I don't think so, but I really don't know."

"Was there ever a report about a gunshot?" Declan asked. "You were probably too young to remember."

"There was always gunshots. My pops would make me hide under my bed or in the tub. I remember that. The neighborhood has changed from the way it was back then. It's a much nicer place to live now. I guess that's good because it's so close to the college campus."

"I have one more question. Do you know if your father was ever contacted by the other victim's family?" Declan asked.

"Not that I know of," he responded. "My pops had left the job after that Ragland lady died. He never wanted to talk about it, but I could just tell. He felt terrible. I think he even felt like he was responsible for her—that he failed to protect her."

"Jeremiah, why are you convinced that Ezra was murdered?" Declan inquired.

"I know my dad. He wouldn't've killed hisself like that. He hated guns. The one they found in the house wasn't his. He never owned one."

When they left the house, Everleigh asked, "Are you thinking that Ezra Stone was killed by the same person who wants to hurt me and Rae? You look like you believe Jeremiah."

"It's worth investigating," Declan said.

"My grandfather must have told him about me. That must be how these people found out about me. That's the only answer."

"I requested a copy of Ezra's file," he announced. "I'm picking it up in an hour."

"What a burden for him to feel responsible for what happened to my mom and Olivia. It wasn't his fault."

Declan nodded in agreement. "But I can understand why he'd feel that way."

"He was a protector," Everleigh said.

"There is the possibility that Jeremiah's right and he was murdered. If so, what was the motive?"

"One possible motive is because he couldn't save Olivia that night," she responded. "If we're right and one of her children is behind this… He rented her the apartment where the previous tenant was attacked. This is what you're thinking, right?"

"It's all speculation, but we might as well consider all possibilities," he replied.

"In the meantime, I plan to look into Olivia's sons. I want to know everything there is to know about them."

"If it's them, then we already know that they grew up to be very angry men with a lust for vengeance."

"And blood."

Everleigh had retired to her hotel room to rest after such a fraught morning. Declan went to his own room to read a copy of Ezra Stone's file. He spread the contents of the folder across the king-size bed.

There was a photo of Ezra slumped in a tattered, brown leather chair next to an equally worn couch, his legs thrust out in front of him, arms limp at his sides. His head drooped on his chest, blood leaking down the side of his face from a bullet hole in his left temple.

Declan looked at another photograph of the room that had been taken at a different angle.

"Did you find anything interesting?" Everleigh asked when she knocked on his door thirty minutes later.

"I'm not sure," he responded. "It certainly looks like he died by suicide, from a gunshot to the temple."

"Looks can be deceiving," she murmured. "Could someone have set the scene up to look like that after they killed him?"

"It's possible," Declan mused. "From everything we've learned about him, like how he hated guns I don't believe he was suicidal, either. So do you still hold to your theory that Ezra may have been killed by one or both of the Ragland brothers because they blamed him for what happened to Olivia, or they thought he would have information about the previous occupant…my mother?"

"We've been assuming no one knew your mother had

been attacked in the apartment because she didn't tell anyone. But Ezra found out from your grandfather."

She let out a frustrated sigh. "I wish we had solid proof. Right now, we're just pulling at loose threads. We may not have any real answers until it's too late."

"Powell lived in Villa Rica for a while," Declan said. "I saw somewhere that he lived there with a cousin. I think the name was Mattie Powell. If she's still around, maybe she'll be willing to talk to us."

Everleigh pulled out her iPad. "Let's see what we can find about her online."

She was determined to help him with this investigation. He'd allowed her to do so to keep Everleigh from going rogue on her own.

Declan finished off a bottle of water.

"I found her. According to this, she still lives in Villa Rica." Everleigh took a screenshot of the information. "Just texted it to you."

"I'll head out to see her tomorrow morning," he said.

Everleigh gave a slight nod. "Maybe she'll be able to tell you something useful."

"If she received a letter, that will certainly help," Declan responded. "We need more proof that a killer is targeting the Powell family."

"I'm going with you," Everleigh announced the next morning.

"Are you sure you want to do that?" Declan had been under the impression that she wasn't interested in meeting any members of Powell's family.

"Yes. Only, she doesn't have to know that I'm a relative."

"If you're sure," he said.

"I am," she responded.

"What about Rae?"

"Bonnie wants to take Rae to a birthday party this afternoon. She said she'd drop her off at the hotel afterward."

"Let's head out then," he said.

They got into the car and headed toward I-20 West.

Declan glanced over at her. She was twirling her rings around her finger. "Are you okay?"

Everleigh nodded. "I am. I don't know why I'm feeling so nervous."

"You're about to meet a member of your family on your father's side—only you don't want them to know it. I'm sure anyone would feel a certain amount of stress in that situation."

"I guess I'm curious," she said. "I think I need to see someone from that family who is not a killer. This probably doesn't make sense."

"Actually, it does," he responded. "I'd feel the same way. You need someone outside of Powell as a point of reference for your paternal side."

He parked on the street in front of a ranch-style brick home forty-five minutes later.

"You ready to do this?" Declan asked before getting out of the car.

"As ready as I'll ever be," she replied.

They got out and climbed the steps to the porch.

"The door isn't closed all the way," Everleigh said, touching his arm.

Declan examined it. "Looks like it was forced open. You stay out here."

"No," she responded. "I'm staying right behind you."

"Mattie Powell…" he called out.

There was no answer.

He stepped inside with Everleigh following closely behind.

"Stay here by the door," Declan instructed in a whisper. "I have a really bad feeling."

She nodded.

His weapon in his hand, Declan moved silently down the hallway. It was so quiet in the house that the only sounds he heard were the muffled thuds of his boots on the carpet and the ticking of a clock on a nightstand through an open bedroom door.

A woman was in bed, lying on her side.

"Mattie…"

She didn't move, but Declan didn't really expect she would. From where he stood at the door, he could tell she was dead.

"We have to call the police," he said, holstering his weapon as he returned to the front of the house. "Mattie's dead. She was shot in the head. From the looks of it, she was sleeping—she didn't see it coming."

"I guess that's a small blessing," Everleigh replied. She shuddered.

They waited outside on the porch.

"How long do you think she's been dead?" Everleigh asked.

"At least twelve hours."

Everleigh suddenly looked fearful. "The killer may still be in the area. I think we should leave."

The whine of a siren sounded in the distance, followed by the blare of a second vehicle. "Here they come," Declan said, pulling out his credentials.

"That didn't take long at all," Everleigh responded. "What do we tell them?"

"That we came looking for information about Powell."

Two patrol cars pulled up to the house.

An officer took their statement while the other three entered the house.

"Did you know the victim?"

"No, we didn't," Declan replied.

"Then what were you doing here?" the officer asked.

"We wanted to talk to Mattie about her cousin," Everleigh said. "I thought she might have some information about James Ray Powell."

"The medical examiner is on her way now," another officer said from the doorway.

Declan answered more of the officer's questions, and so did Everleigh.

When the homicide detective arrived, he and Declan walked off to the side to talk.

"Someone's threatened Mrs. Taylor and her child. We were in Atlanta to try to narrow down potential suspects. We drove out here to see Mattie Powell and found her body."

"How is your investigation connected to the victim?"

Declan looked back at Everleigh.

The resigned expression on her face told him that she knew what had to happen next. She walked over to where they were standing.

"The person who is after me believes that Powell is my father. I wanted to meet Mattie to find out more about him."

"Several of his family members have been killed," Declan said. "Two by gunshot and one was bludgeoned to death. I also believe there are two assailants."

"Any suspects?"

"Two brothers. Ellis and Neil Ragland. Their mother was Olivia Ragland, who was a victim of Powell's." He took out a business card and handed it to the police officer. "We're staying at the Peachtree Hotel downtown. You can have the detective contact me. I'm sure he or she will have some questions as well."

"How long will you be in town?"

"We plan to leave tomorrow afternoon."

"Someone will be in touch."

Declan placed his arm around Everleigh as they walked to the car.

"That poor woman. They're running around killing innocent people. They aren't any better than Powell." She looked up at him. "If they're here, do you think they've given up on me?"

"I wish I could say yeah, but the truth is that I don't think so, Everleigh. They may have moved on, but they'll be back. These people are bloodthirsty killers."

"I know you're right," she said. "As much as I don't want to believe it. What I want most is to find them before they find me. I'm sick of this cat-and-mouse game."

He hadn't heard her talk like this before. She wasn't anyone's victim. Everleigh was a fighter. A survivor.

"Why are you looking at me like that?"

Holding the passenger side door open for her, Declan said, "You're literally fighting mad right now. *I love it.*"

Everleigh laughed as she slid inside. "I guess I am. I'm more like my mother than I realized. She was a bear when it came to protecting me. Just the thought of two angry men wanting to harm my daughter—I want to put some serious hurt on them."

When he got in on the driver's side, he said, "Maybe I should worry about protecting Neil and Ellis from *you.*"

"By locking them behind bars, I hope," she responded.

"Best place for them," Declan stated.

They started the drive back to the hotel.

En route he received a phone call.

"That was a Detective Bell. He and his partner are the lead investigators on Mattie Powell's case. They're coming to the hotel to talk to us."

"I'll order some food when we get there," Everleigh said. "I'm not hungry, but I know Rae will want something when Bonnie drops her off. I'll order enough for the detectives, too."

"He said they would be here in about an hour," Declan told her.

"I know I have to tell them the truth about my relationship to Powell. I just hope that they won't blab it to the world."

"We can ask that they keep it out of the reports," he said. "And hopefully, they will honor it."

"I guess there's nothing we can do about it if they don't," Everleigh responded.

He reached out and took her hand. "Everything is going to be okay."

She nodded in agreement. "I do believe that. I would just like to focus on making sure Rae enjoys the holidays. She's just a little girl."

Declan glanced over at her. "She's going to have that, Everleigh. I intend to make sure of it."

They made small talk during the rest of the drive.

After parking the car, Declan and Everleigh took the elevator up to her hotel room.

She ordered an assortment of sandwiches.

They sat down on the couch to wait for their food and the detectives to arrive.

"What if we were seen at Mattie's house?" Everleigh asked.

"By who?"

"By the person responsible for her death."

"The only other people who drove down that dirt road was the police. Her house is pretty secluded."

"You're right. I guess my mind is all over the place." She stood up and strode over to the only window in the room.

"Are you okay?" he asked.

She didn't answer right away, but instead turned to the window, her fingers tracing the contours of the curtains.

Mattie's death had affected Everleigh, despite her attempts to remain composed. She bit her lower lip and turned to face him, looking into his eyes. "I don't know what I would have done if I didn't have you to lean on."

He leaned down and kissed her gently, a moment of pause in their tumultuous lives that caught them both by surprise.

The kiss was broken by a knock on the door.

"They're here," Declan said softly.

Everleigh took a deep breath and murmured, "Let's get this over with."

Everleigh had no time to process what had just happened between her and Declan. The detectives were there to question them regarding Mattie Powell. There wasn't much they could tell him about her death specifically— only their suspicions.

Declan let the detectives inside the room. "We ordered some sandwiches," he said. "There's coffee and soft drinks."

The men exchanged glances. "It's been a long morning," said the one who introduced himself as Howard Bell. "I could use something to eat. But I'd prefer to take care of business first."

Everleigh sat down on the sofa beside Declan as the homicide detectives sat across from them in chairs.

"I understand you're a criminal investigator from Charleston. What was the reason for your visit to Mattie Powell?" Bell asked.

"Everleigh received a threatening letter dated six months ago and she came to me for help," Declan stated. "The person who sent it believes that she's Powell's daughter."

"*Are* you James Ray Powell's daughter?" Bell asked.

"Yes." It galled her to have to admit that horrible truth.

"She doesn't want anyone to know," Declan interjected. "So I'm hoping you will keep it away from the public."

Everleigh stood up when a knock sounded. "That must be room service."

"My mother was one of his victims," Everleigh clarified after signing the check and seeing the server to the door. "She never reported it. She didn't know his identity until months later after he was arrested."

Bell nodded in understanding. "We'll do our best to keep it out of the case, Mrs. Taylor."

"That's all I ask," she stated. "Thank you."

"I'm sure this is a stretch, but do you happen to have that letter with you?" Bell's partner, Detective Larry Rowe, inquired.

"I have a picture of it," Everleigh responded.

"She gave the original to me," Declan said. "I had it tested for prints but the results yielded nothing."

"There was a letter similar to this on her nightstand," Rowe announced.

Everleigh gasped. She glanced over at Declan, who looked just as surprised.

"Was it dated about six months ago?" he asked.

"Yes. We're not releasing that information to the public, so we ask that you keep it to yourself."

Declan gave a small nod. "Understood."

Everleigh pointed to the silver tray heaped with neatly halved sandwiches after the server delivered them to the room. "Please help yourselves. What would you like to drink? Water, coffee or soda?"

"I'll take water," said Bell.

"I'll have coffee," his partner responded.

Everyone helped themselves to the food, and they ate

in silence for a while. When they were finished, the detectives rose.

"We have what we need," Rowe said.

Declan shook their hands. "I would really appreciate your keeping me informed about the investigation."

"We ask that you do the same," Bell replied.

"Are we free to leave Atlanta?" Everleigh asked.

"Yes, ma'am," Larry responded.

Everleigh looked over at Declan when the detectives left. "Do you think they'll keep their word?"

"I think they will do as they said—they will try to keep the information out of their investigation. It shouldn't be a problem because your being Powell's daughter shouldn't come into play. It has nothing to do with Mattie's murder."

"But when Ellis and Neil are caught, it will get out because it provides motive," Everleigh said. "I'll deal with it when the time comes."

THIRTEEN

Everleigh played a reading game with her daughter that night while Declan made a visit to the Atlanta police precinct.

She'd already packed their bags since they were leaving first thing in the morning. She was actually looking forward to going home. Everleigh planned to tell Declan on the way back to Charleston that she and Rae were going back to their house. When Ellis and Neil came for her, she'd be ready.

"Mama, where's Mr. Declan?"

"He had to run an errand," Everleigh responded. "He should be back soon."

"I like him."

She smiled. "I know you do, sweetie. You know what? I like him, too."

"I miss Billie. I bet she misses me, too."

"Yes, she does."

They finished their game, so they moved on to a round of Go Fish.

Every time they heard a sound outside, they both stared at the door expectantly.

They were both looking forward to seeing Declan. Everleigh hoped he would be arriving any moment now. She didn't mind Rae's attachment to him, but she didn't want her to see Declan as a father figure—only as a friend.

Christmas was fast approaching and she still had a few things on her list she wanted to get for Rae. It was going to be the first one without her mom and the second without Britt.

Declan arrived a half hour later.

"We're so glad you're here," Rae declared. "Me and Mama missed you."

Everleigh averted her gaze. She didn't want him getting the wrong idea. She enjoyed his company—that was all it was.

Liar.

The truth was that she cared more for Declan than she ever cared to admit. He'd gotten under her skin and pierced her heart and soul.

"Everything go okay?" she asked.

He gave a slight nod.

Everleigh knew that he would share more once they were able to talk privately. Declan had gone there to see if there was any information on the Ragland brothers in the system. They wanted to know the type of people they were dealing with.

God, I just want to get back to my life. Is this Your way of getting my attention? If so, it worked.

She closed her eyes and sent up a quick prayer.

Declan smiled to himself as he watched Everleigh with Rae. They were laughing and talking about Christmas. The little girl was extremely excited about all the presents she was going to get.

Every now and then, a yawn interrupted Rae's chatter. She was sleepy but kept trying to fight it. Eventually, her exhaustion won out and she was fast asleep.

"She was trying her hardest to hang out with us," Everleigh said when she joined him on the sofa.

"She's adorable," Declan responded. "You're very blessed to have that little girl."

"I know. She's one of the reasons I smile every day." Changing the subject, Everleigh asked, "How did it go at the police station?"

"The Ragland brothers lived for a short time with their father after Olivia's death. He disappeared about a year after, and they were placed in a group home. As I thought, Ellis and Neil are no strangers to violence and criminal activities," Declan said. "The last known address is in Virginia. That was over three years ago, so they can be anywhere."

He handed her a couple of photos. "Neil is the one with the dreadlocks."

"I've never seen either of them before," Everleigh responded. "Ellis looks sinister with that scar on his forehead. I'm pretty sure they're heading back to Charleston."

"If you ever get tired of teaching, you should look into becoming a police detective. You've be good at it."

She laughed.

"I mean it. You have great instincts about people."

"I'll keep that in mind, Declan."

"You know, I sat in during one of your lectures," he said. Her eyebrows rose in surprise. "When was this?"

"A couple of weeks after you started. It was on self-justification in everyday life. I loved what you said about us lying to ourselves daily. We lie about how good or bad we are at the various things we do."

"It's true," Everleigh responded. "Our skewed beliefs infiltrate our day-to-day life so effectively that we rarely notice we're doing it. We can see fault so clearly in others but we're blissfully unaware of them when it comes to our own thoughts and behaviors."

"Why do you think that is?" Declan asked.

"Because facing the lie we tell ourselves would mean redefining how we see ourselves. If the Ragland brothers really are the killers—then they are a prime example of this," she explained. "They believe that they're justified in killing innocent people all because those people are related to James Ray Powell. They don't see themselves as killers. If Powell, Ellis and Neil were to face the truth, they would have to reevaluate themselves and it would be less than flattering. In their case, murderers. All of them. Most people would be unable to live with that label, so playing ostrich is much easier."

Declan could talk with Everleigh all night long, but they had to be up early in the morning. It was time to go home.

They had no idea where the Ragland brothers were, but at least now they knew whom they were dealing with.

"When we get back to Charleston, Rae and I are going back to our house," Everleigh announced the next morning. "I'm not going to stop living my life." One of the first things she planned to do was upgrade her security, this time installing cameras all around her house.

"I can't change your mind?" he asked.

"I've given it a lot of thought, Declan."

"I have to be honest. I'd feel better if you continue staying at my place until we have these guys in custody, but it's your decision. I'll make sure the island police keep an eye on your home."

"Thank you," she said. "I'm tired of hiding, but I don't want to put Rae at risk. However, this is the only way to catch them."

After they made it to Angel Island, Declan walked them

to their front door. Everleigh took Declan's hand. "Come back this evening for dinner, please."

He smiled. "I'd love to join the two most beautiful girls on the island for dinner."

"Great. We'll see you then."

His words left her with a warm feeling in her belly.

When Declan drove away, Everleigh headed back inside and found her daughter in the hallway. "We've got a lot to do this afternoon. We're going to…" Her voice died at the sight of the broken picture frame on the floor.

"Mama, who broke the picture?" Rae asked.

"It must have fallen somehow," she said, but Everleigh knew better. Someone had been inside their home. The tiny hairs on the back of her neck stood to attention.

It had to be Wyle.

Everleigh opened up the app to her security system. She'd unarmed it when they first pulled up into the driveway. She was sure of it. After checking out Rae's room, she told her, "You stay in here. I'll come get you when I'm ready to get started. Okay?"

She locked the door when she left the room. Taser in hand, Everleigh went from room to room, checking closets, bathrooms—she checked the house from top to bottom.

Satisfied that no one was in the house, she opened her security app again and did a more thorough review. She felt a chill run through her when she saw that her system had been disarmed while she was at Declan's house. Wyle had a background in IT and Everleigh believed that he'd hacked her alarm.

She called her security company and changed the credentials. Next, she called Officer Lee and filed a report.

He came to the house almost immediately. She kept Rae busy while he did a walk-through, and she shared her suspicions about Wyle, how he'd been in her yard and how he had the means to disarm her security system.

When he left, Everleigh went online to purchase a second security system as a backup until she could change companies.

She took a moment to thank God that she and Rae had not been here at the time of the home invasion.

Everleigh briefly considered Declan's offer to stay with him. "No, I'm not doing that," she whispered. "I'm not going to let him run me out of my home."

"What you say, Mama?"

"Nothing, sweetie. I'm just rambling."

"Why?"

She chuckled. "I have no idea."

"Mama, you're so silly."

Everleigh embraced Rae. "I love you to pieces."

"I love you, too."

They spent the next couple of hours cooking together, and then they went upstairs to get ready for dinner.

Everleigh chose a sapphire-blue sweater dress and paired it with cognac-colored boots. Rae chose a navy dress to wear with her camel cowboy boots.

"Mama, wear your hair just like it is," Rae instructed.

Everleigh eyed her reflection in the mirror. Her hair was a mass of loose curls. She spritzed it with water and leave-in conditioner to tame the frizz.

Ten minutes later, Declan arrived.

She led him into the dining room.

He eyed the table, which she and Rae had decorated, and asked, "You did all this?"

Everleigh nodded. "Rae and I wanted to do something special for you."

"You succeeded."

Vibrant flames in red and gold flickered from the silver-colored candles, casting a soft glow on the succulent display of baked chicken, roasted potatoes, yeast rolls and steaming broccoli.

"Everything looks delicious," he said.

"Thank you," she murmured as she sat down in the chair he had pulled out for her. He did the same for Rae.

Declan walked around the table and eased into a chair facing her. "Did you cook all this?"

She nodded. "I did."

"And I *helped*," Rae interjected. "I made the *brock-li*."

Grinning, he said, "You did a great job, too."

"Me and Mama made brownies for dessert," Rae announced. "Chocolate peanut-butter."

Declan awarded them a smile. "I want you to know that this is much appreciated."

After dinner, Everleigh told Rae she could go watch television. With just the adults at the table, Declan said, "I've never met a woman like you. I haven't met anyone who would do something like this for a man they barely know."

Everleigh pushed away from the table. "I enjoy giving flowers to people while they can see and smell them, Declan. Life is too short—I don't take any day for granted."

He got up from the table and followed her into the kitchen.

Declan touched a finger to her chin. His eyes were bright with an emotion she couldn't identify.

His mouth curved up at the corners. His finger brushed against Everleigh's skin, moving back and forth, making it difficult for her to think.

He kissed her.

"I just don't think it's a good idea for us to get carried away," she murmured against his cheek before stepping back.

Their gazes locked and Everleigh moved forward again, letting him wrap his arms around her. He gazed into her eyes.

Everleigh drew his face to hers.

He kissed her again, lingering, savoring every moment.

Everleigh's emotions whirled. Blood pounded in her brain, leaped from her heart and made her knees tremble.

"Thank you," he whispered.

Puzzled, she asked, "For what?"

"For trusting me."

She smiled at him. "Thank you for being a friend to me, Declan. And for your protection."

"It's my honor, Everleigh."

"I thought we was watching a movie," Rae called from the family room.

"Here we come," she said, taking Declan's hand in her own.

When his gaze landed on the broken frame, Everleigh whispered, "It's nothing to worry about. I've already ordered a new one."

"What happened?"

"We found it on the floor broken when we came home earlier."

Declan's eyes didn't leave her face.

"I think Wyle... I know he was in our house while we were staying with you. But you don't have to worry. The security system have been changed and I've installed a backup security system—I have cameras everywhere now. Plus, a locksmith is on the way."

"Did you have a police officer come out?"

"I filed a report with Officer Lee. He came out and did a walk-through. Wyle came in through the back door."

"You should've called me," he said.

"You'd just gotten home. I knew that you were tired."

"I really don't like leaving you and Rae alone in this house."

"Declan, this is our home," Everleigh stated. "I won't let some stranger run me away from it like Powell did my mother."

"Leaving is what saved her life."

He was right, of course.

FOURTEEN

Declan was touched beyond measure by the lengths Everleigh went through to make the evening special for him. An invisible thread was pulling them closer and closer. But at the moment, he was still upset with her for not telling him immediately about the break-in.

Everleigh was trying to be brave, but it was also making her a bit reckless. How could he protect them if she didn't keep him informed of any threats? He considered staking out her house after he left for the evening, but he decided against it. He had to be at the precinct early, and Lee was parked outside the house. Declan would speak briefly with him before he left the island.

The next morning, he was at his desk at the precinct when his phone began vibrating, taking him out of his musings.

It was Detective Bell.

He pressed the button to answer. "Declan Blanchet speaking."

"I wanted to let you know that a vehicle belonging to Ellis Ragland received a ticket in Charleston two days ago."

Their hunch was right. The Ragland brothers were involved, and as he'd hoped, they'd made a mistake.

There wasn't anything new on Mattie's death. They talked a few minutes more before hanging up.

He let out a frustrated sigh, then called Everleigh. Declan hated having to give her this piece of news. They both knew this day would come…but he'd prayed for divine intervention in this situation.

There was no answer.

His muscles rigid and his jaw clenched, Declan left his desk and headed out. He was going to the house to make sure Everleigh and Rae were okay. He knew what the Ragland brothers were capable of and he didn't want to take any chances.

One of his coworkers approached him, but Declan responded in a rushed tone. He didn't have time to socialize. He was in a hurry to get to Angel Island.

It wasn't like Everleigh to not answer her phone.

He walked with haste out of the precinct and jumped into his car. He tried her again. "C'mon, Everleigh. Answer your phone."

No answer. A wave of apprehension snaked down his spine.

Declan rubbed the back of his neck while he drove, trying to stay mindful of the speed limit, praying for smooth traffic and the safety of Everleigh and Rae. Declan had promised to protect them and he didn't want to break his word.

"I can't fail them," he said to the empty car. "Lord, please keep them safe."

With hot coffee fresh from the pot, the latest edition of the *American Journal of Psychology* spread out on her kitchen island and pajamas still enrobing her fatigued body, Everleigh slowly devoured a spinach, mushroom and tomato omelet as she read an article without interruption.

After she finished off her omelet, she went upstairs to wake Rae.

"Hey, sweetie…it's time to get up."

"Mama, I'm hungry. I was dreaming about food all night."

"Oh, really? What kinds of food?"

"Choc'late cake, hot dogs, hamburgers and chicken."

"I see. Well, you can't have any of that for breakfast. So what do you think you'd like instead?"

"Choc'late-chip waffles, bacon and fruit."

"That's doable," Everleigh said. "C'mon, get up and head straight to the bathroom."

"It's almost Christmas, Mama."

She planted a kiss on her daughter's forehead. "I know… it's less than a week away."

Everleigh had breakfast waiting for Rae when she came downstairs. She cleaned the kitchen while her daughter ate, then Rae went up to her bedroom to play.

Everleigh saw the mail carrier turn onto her street from the window. She was expecting a package—a Christmas gift she'd ordered for Rae, which was due to arrive any day now. She opened the door while her daughter was upstairs, so that Rae wouldn't hear and come down to investigate.

Everleigh had taken only a few steps onto the porch when a tall, broad-shouldered man stepped out from behind the hedge. The look on his face was ominous, and the scar above his right eye made him look menacing.

He lunged toward her, grabbing her arm and dragging her onto the porch.

She had the presence of mind to swallow her scream. Everleigh didn't want to scare Rae. With her heart pounding, she struggled to break free.

Pain ripped down her arm as she wrenched it away from him. "Keep your hands off me."

Pointing a gun at her, he demanded lowly, "Don't make

a scene. Just march into the house like you would any other day."

Lifting her chin in defiance, she uttered, "I wouldn't have a gun at my back if this were *any other day.*"

"Shut up." His angry voice spiked the fear swirling around within her.

"I know who you are… Ellis Ragland. Listen, I don't have anything to do with James Ray Powell. I only found out a few months ago that he's my father. How did you find out?"

"You can thank your friend Wyle Gaines," he sneered. "We were at a bar minding our business when we happened to hear this guy complaining to anyone who would listen about the serial-killer spawn who cheated him out of a fortune. It won't surprise you that I'm interested in serial killers, so I got to talking with him. He told us everything about you—all we had to do was get him drinking. Imagine our surprise when it turned out which serial-killer family did him wrong."

"Why are you doing this?" she asked.

"It's because of your mother that mine died."

Everleigh shook her head. "That's not true."

"Powell went to that apartment looking for *your* mother," he said. "It's *her* fault."

"My mom died—there's nothing you can do to her. I understand that you want to blame someone, but that person is Powell and he's already behind bars."

"That's not enough payment for what I had to go through," Ellis huffed.

"My mother was a victim. I'm not connected to that serial killer and neither is my daughter. I'm sure your mother wouldn't want you to do this."

"I have to do it. There's a serial-killer gene," he said. "Did you know that? I expect you should since you're a shrink. Once we heard how you'd mistreated ol' Wyle, I looked up your mama. That's how we found out about the apartment. That's when we decided everyone with Powell's evil blood needed to die."

"Ellis, you need to know that there's no *serial-killer* gene," Everleigh stated.

"Sure there is. I've heard podcasts about it. Did you know that one of Powell's uncles was also a killer? The coward took his own life before he could be apprehended."

"It's not true. However, there is a gene that can influence a person's level of aggression and emotional control."

"Don't try to trick me…"

"I'm not," she responded, her voice wavering. "I'm telling you the truth. That serial-killer theory was debunked— it's nothing more than a myth."

He shook his head. "Naw… I don't believe you."

She tried to keep from trembling as she spoke. "You can check on the internet," Everleigh stated. "I wouldn't lie to you."

"Get inside," he ordered, glancing around suspiciously.

Everleigh hesitated, fear and doubt mixing in her mind as she thought about protecting her daughter from him. "Ellis, you don't want to do this…"

He rounded on her with anger flashing in his eyes. "Stop trying to tell me what I want or don't want," he snapped.

"I'm sorry. I'm not trying to upset you. You have to understand that hurting me…hurting my daughter… I'm telling you that it won't matter to Powell. He doesn't even know we exist."

"You're his blood. I need to eliminate you."

"Look, there's a police cruiser about to turn on this street. He's going to stop here."

Ellis turned his head away from her.

Everleigh flexed her wrist and took a step toward him,

aiming for his nose. She used the momentary distraction to her advantage and did a high kick, knocking the gun out of Ellis's hand.

He shoved her down in his effort to recover his weapon.

As she fell to the ground, she heard pounding footsteps.

Ellis tried to run away, but the yard was soon covered with police officers.

She heard Declan's voice, but didn't see him. All Everleigh wanted to do was get to Rae.

"His gun is over there," she told one of the officers.

"This isn't over," Ellis hissed at her.

"Please get him out of my yard. I don't want my daughter seeing this man."

Declan walked over to her. "Are you okay?"

Everleigh nodded. "I'm fine."

"Why didn't you answer your phone? I called you at least four times."

She looked down at her pajamas. "No pockets. I think my phone's in my bedroom." She looked up at Declan. "How did you know to come here?"

"Bell called and told me that Ellis got a ticket a couple days ago in Charleston. I was riding over here to tell you about that. But when you didn't answer, I got worried. I called the island precinct."

"I'm fine. I just want them to get him away from my house." Everleigh started shivering uncontrollably.

Declan gathered Everleigh into his arms, holding her close. He was relieved to find that she and Rae hadn't been harmed. He didn't want to think of the alternative.

She stirred slightly. "I'm so glad you got here when you did. And the police. Ellis was trying to force me inside the house. I guess he'd planned to kill us there."

"Where's Rae?" Declan inquired.

"She's in the house," she responded. "She was upstairs when I was on my way to check my mail. I really hope she didn't see any of this. I need to check on her."

"Try to keep her away from the windows."

Everleigh nodded.

When she returned a few minutes later, she said, "Thank goodness, Rae had gone back to sleep. Looks like she missed everything."

"I see you're very capable of handling yourself," Declan said, "But you shouldn't take any unnecessary risks. Ellis and his brother are *killers*."

"All that was on my mind is that I had to do whatever I could to protect my child," Everleigh responded. "Rae is who I was thinking about at the time." She paused a moment, then said, "Neil is still out there somewhere."

"We'll find him."

"What if he doesn't have anything to do with this?"

"Once we locate him, we'll know for sure," Declan said.

"I want to know everything there is about these men," Everleigh insisted.

"I do, too. In the meantime, I don't think it's safe for you to stay here."

He was relieved when she nodded in agreement. She said, "I was thinking the same thing. I guess I should find a hotel—"

"No, I have the perfect place. It's safe and away from Charleston. My sister is in Europe for a couple of months and her house in Columbia, South Carolina, is empty. I'd planned on spending the holidays there. You and Rae can join me."

"I've tried so hard to make this place a home for Rae and me. I hate to leave it, even for a little while." She bit her lip. "But we can be ready within the hour."

* * *

Neil watched the police take his brother away. He'd warned him against confronting Everleigh like this, but Ellis never listened to him.

He knew his brother would never give him up. Ellis would take it upon himself to spend time in prison alone rather than give Neil up. He'd always protected him, even when they were in that foster home. He nearly killed the man who'd been abusing him when he tried to touch Neil. They ran away and lived on the streets for months before they were picked up and taken to a group home.

Neil owed Ellis his life. He always willingly suffered the brunt of the abuse they endured. Whenever other kids used to tease him about his stutter, Ellis would step up and make them stop.

I won't abandon you now.

But he couldn't just show up at the precinct. Since the police had Ellis in custody, there was a chance that they also knew about him. If he wasn't careful, it would only be a matter of time before he was behind bars with his brother.

Neil was determined to find a way to get Ellis out. Once again, he'd have to put his dreams on hold.

I can do that for my brother. He needs me more.

A part of him wanted to stay to see what would happen next, but Neil changed his mind when two more cruisers pulled up to the house.

With so many police officers in the area, he decided to return to the motel in Charleston.

"Are we going on another trip?" Rae asked when Everleigh woke her. She sat up, rubbing her eyes. "I was still tired so I laid down."

"We're going away...yes." Everleigh's words came out

in a rush. "I've already packed your bag. Grab your hat and coat."

"Mama, where're we going?"

"Sweetie, just do as I asked. We need to hurry."

Declan appeared in the bedroom doorway. "Rae, why don't I help you with your backpack," he said. "Let's see if we can get to the car before your mom."

The little girl grinned. "Yeah. I'm real fast."

Everleigh gave him a grateful smile.

She went back to her room to see if she'd forgotten anything she might need while she was away. Everleigh made sure she had her cell phone, laptop and iPad, plus all her charging cords. She made a quick call to Robin to let her know that she was going to have deliveries routed to her house temporarily.

When she walked out of the house ten minutes later, she found Rae seated inside Declan's car, Declan standing beside the open trunk.

Everleigh glanced around before sliding into the front passenger seat. She didn't notice anything out of the ordinary. She released a soft sigh of relief that she and Rae were going away. It was clear that they were no longer safe.

During the drive, Declan asked Everleigh, "How you holding up?"

She glanced back at Rae, who was wearing a headset. She seemed engrossed in the movie she was watching on her tablet.

"He came to my house to kill me."

"I'm sorry," Declan responded.

Everleigh shivered at the very thought of Ellis being that close to her. She was always intentional about safety, but somehow, she'd missed him lurking nearby.

"Ellis is locked up now."

"True, but his brother is still out there. If Neil's involved, he won't be able to get to us right now, but we can't stay away forever. Declan, I'm not going to live my life on the run. I just wanted Rae to have her first Christmas here in our new house."

"I understand," he said. "I'm optimistic that Neil will be found soon—especially if he's in Charleston."

"I have confidence in you and the police department. I guess I shouldn't have waited this long to get them involved."

"You were trying to stay out of the spotlight and keep your daughter safe."

"I found out how Ellis and Neil found out about me," Everleigh said. "Wyle Gaines. They overheard him talking about me in a bar, by complete coincidence." She shuddered. "He was supposed to be my mother's friend. I can't believe my mother would confide in him, but she did."

"Mama, I'm hungry."

Everleigh glanced back at Rae and smiled. "We're almost there. I put a sandwich and fruit in the bag beside you."

"Thank you."

"You're welcome, sweetie."

"Never in a million years did I think we'd be spending the holidays together," Declan said with a chuckle, steering the conversation to a lighter topic.

"I didn't see this coming, either."

"I'm glad to have this chance to get to know you, though."

She smiled. "Same here."

Everleigh was sincere about getting to know Declan. He had a great sense of humor and made her laugh. Something she hadn't really done in a while. He also made her feel emotions she thought had died with Britt. Emotions that betrayed her love for him. Everleigh knew that there was nothing wrong with moving on and finding love a second time, but she didn't want to chance it with Declan. She couldn't bear the loss. It would be too much.

It's not healthy to think this way. Everleigh wasn't a pessimist, but she preferred to face reality because it kept her from the hope of something more where Declan was concerned.

FIFTEEN

Declan was dealing with his own feelings for Everleigh. She had an infectious laugh that he loved. She was intelligent, courageous and beautiful—not to mention a loving mother to Rae. But he couldn't forget that she still wore her wedding rings. A sure sign that she was still grieving the loss of her husband.

He drove around for a while to make sure they weren't being followed when they arrived in Columbia, South Carolina.

"Are you from Columbia?" Everleigh asked.

Declan nodded. "Born and raised. I attended college in Charleston. Fell in love with the city and decided to make it my home."

"This will be my first time here."

"It has kind of a small-town feel to it," Declan said. "But there are a lot of nice restaurants, culture and art."

"That's nice to know but I'm hoping we'll only be here for a few days. You keep coming to my rescue. I honestly never thought things would get so crazy. Now you're mixed up in this."

"It's not a problem. I probably wouldn't have gotten to know you otherwise."

Everleigh eyed him. "Do you really believe that?"

Declan smiled. "Before this, I couldn't get anything out of you other than a hello."

"You must have thought I was unapproachable."

"Actually, I just assumed you were getting adjusted to the university. I never took it personally."

She smiled. "I'm really glad you didn't. I was focused on making sure Rae was okay and trying to process my grief."

"I understand."

Twenty minutes later, Declan turned on Lakeshore Drive.

"Oh, wow, this house is gorgeous," Everleigh murmured when he pulled into the circular driveway.

"This is the main house, where you'll be staying," he announced.

"Main house?"

"There's a one-bedroom apartment over the four-car garage. There's a guest residence on the property as well."

He led her up the steps to the main house.

"We're staying in here?" Everleigh asked. "Maybe you should put us in the apartment or the guest house?"

"I'll be staying in the apartment. My nephew currently lives in the guesthouse. In fact, he should be arriving shortly."

Chilly air kissed her skin as soon as she stepped inside. Everleigh pulled the folds of her coat together.

"I just turned on the heat," he said. "My sister's been away for a couple of weeks."

Her cold face warmed up at the sight of the gorgeous marble fireplace in the living room. This seemed like the perfect place to enjoy family gatherings or spend quiet evenings with a book.

All the rooms in the house were oversized. She fell in love instantly with the gourmet kitchen that was built to entertain. Nearly every room in the house seemed to offer generous views of the lake. The well-appointed great room also featured a wet bar and high ceilings.

Everleigh couldn't resist stepping out onto the large covered porch that overlooked a saltwater pool, a cabana and the lake.

Rae joined her. "Mama, I like this house."

"So do I, sweetie. It's beautiful and very peaceful."

"Yeah."

Declan went to put his car in an empty space in the garage.

Upon his return, he said, "I put you and Rae in the bedroom down here. I figured you'd be more comfortable with having her in the same room."

"Thank you." Everleigh's gaze traveled her surroundings. "Is this the master bedroom?"

"It's one of two. There's another upstairs," Declan explained. "That's my sister's."

"I'm glad to hear that," Everleigh said. "Because I didn't want to invade her personal space."

A man who looked to be in his mid-twenties walked into the house.

"This is my nephew, Remy," Declan said.

"It's nice to meet you," Everleigh murmured, noting the police-academy hoodie he wore beneath his leather jacket.

"And you as well." He also shared the same eyes and full lips as Declan, and like his uncle, Remy sported a neatly trimmed mustache and beard.

Holding out her hand to him, Rae introduced herself.

He grinned. "It's nice to meet you, Rae. I have a little girl about your age. Her name is Halle. She's four years old."

"I'm five. Can I meet her?"

"You sure can. She's actually coming for a visit tomorrow. She'll be here until after the New Year." To Everleigh, he said, "My wife is finishing up school in North Carolina—graduating in May. After that, they'll be living here full-time."

"That's wonderful," Everleigh said.

"Did you notice anyone following us?" Declan asked.

"No, I was about three vehicles behind you once you entered the city," Remy responded. "I hung back to see if anyone followed you from the exit to the house."

"I didn't see anyone, either, but I didn't want to chance it without a set of second eyes."

Everleigh looked over at Declan. "You arranged all this?"

He nodded. "I promised to keep you safe."

"Did you show her the panic room?" Remy asked.

"Not yet."

Her eyes widened in surprise. "There's a panic room?"

"It's in the library, which is beside the room you and Rae will be staying in. I'll show it to you later. I'm pretty sure you won't be needing it because no one knows you're here. Plus, Remy and I will be around. You'll never be alone. One of us will always be close by."

Remy gave her an encouraging smile. "My mom said for you to make yourself comfortable and she looks forward to meeting you in the future."

Everleigh smiled back. "Please convey my gratitude to her."

Declan took them on a tour around the ten-acre property. "This land belonged to our grandparents," he said. "See that house over there?"

When Everleigh glanced in the direction of Declan's pointing finger and nodded, Declan continued, "That's where my grandparents lived. My dad was born in that house. When he got married, he built what we now call the guesthouse. Dad gave it to me when he and Mom bought a condo in Florida. I decided to renovate and update it. I plan to make it my home after I retire. In the meantime, Remy and his family are welcome to live there."

"That's very sweet." Everleigh admired the professionally landscaped grounds. There was a small garden, a fountain and a shaded pergola. She imagined herself strolling across the manicured lawn and sitting in one of the Adirondack chairs by the seawall while drinking a cup of coffee. "I could sit out here for hours just taking in the solitude."

"That's the idea," Declan responded. "This is where I come whenever I feel the need to clear my mind."

"I'm glad Rae will have someone to play with while we're here." Everleigh looked at him. "You've thought of everything, haven't you?"

"I tried."

"Declan, I want to apologize to you. I should have told you about the break-in as soon as I realized what had taken place. I think it was my pride. I didn't want to fall apart and become a victim. If I'd told you, maybe none of this would be happening right now."

"I have to be honest and say that I'm glad you and Rae are spending time with me," he admitted.

"You have such a way of putting my mind at ease."

Declan smiled. "There's no way Neil or Wyle can find you here. However, I would advise that you not use any credit cards—not even your debit card. If you need cash, I can give it to you."

"I keep cash for emergencies in a safe at home. I brought it with me, so I should be fine," Everleigh replied. She couldn't stop herself from yawning. She was suddenly feeling tired and sleepy.

"Why don't you take a nap?" Declan suggested when they were back inside the house. "Rae can keep me company while I make dinner."

"Are you sure?"

He nodded.

Everleigh walked down the hallway to the bedroom.

As soon as she climbed into the bed, her eyelids felt heavy. She'd been up since 5:00 a.m. and after her run-in with Ellis, Everleigh sought to escape the trauma if only for a short while.

"I can't wait for Halle to get here," Rae said as she ripped a slice of bread apart and tossed it into a bowl. "She's gonna be my friend." She sat at the counter while Declan stood on the other side facing her.

"I have a feeling the two of you are going to be great friends," he responded. Her curly ponytail bobbed up and down with Rae's every move.

"Mr. Declan, how is Santa gonna find me and Halle? We're not at home. He won't be able to find this house because there's no lights, no tree—there's nothing."

"Don't you worry. Remy and I will make sure Santa knows exactly where to find you two."

"I really don't wanna miss Christmas. It's Jesus's birthday."

"You won't," he promised.

"My daddy's in heaven. So is my grandma," Rae stated. "Maybe they'll tell God to make sure I don't miss it."

Declan chuckled. She was such a sweet and adorable little girl. If he was ever blessed with a daughter, he wanted her to be like Rae and Halle. They were both precious.

"The bread's all tore up."

"Good job." He then instructed her on what to do next.

Rae was a good listener and she followed his directions perfectly. "You're going to be a great cook when you grow up."

"I know," she responded. "'Cause Mama teaches me."

He smiled.

"Mr. Declan, I like it out here."

"I'm glad," he responded. "I want you and your mom to have a really nice time while you're here."

She scrunched up her face, then burst into giggles.

"What's that for?" Declan asked with a chuckle.

"I want to see Billie. I miss her. She's a cute doggy."

"I knew I had a surprise for you."

"What is it?"

"Billie will be here tomorrow," he confided. "She's coming with Sherri and Halle." Declan had been in a rush to get Everleigh and Rae out of town—he didn't want to delay the trip by going to get Billie, so he'd arranged for a friend to watch her until Sherri, Remy's wife, could get there. She was also going to pick up the packed duffel he kept in his coat closet for any last-minute trips.

"Yay."

Everleigh walked into the kitchen an hour later, and said, "Something smells delicious."

"Mama, Mr. Declan and I made meat loaf. I got to tear the bread and mix it up in the bowl. It got all squishy." Grinning, she added, "So much fun."

"Smells delicious. I can't wait to taste it."

"You and Rae have a seat," Declan said. "I'll bring everything out."

"Is your nephew joining us?" Everleigh asked.

"Yes. I texted him. He'll be here shortly."

"Declan, from the way all this looks…you're a good cook," Everleigh said.

"Not really. I've only prepared what I know how to make," he confessed.

"Don't let my uncle fool you. He is a great cook," Remy interjected as he took a seat at the table. "He just doesn't like doing it much."

"It's better cooking for others than just myself."

Smiling, Everleigh responded, "I get that. If I didn't have Rae, I'd probably never step into my kitchen. Actually, this isn't true. I enjoy cooking because it calms me."

"Well, I don't have that gift," Remy said. "When my mom is in town, she usually makes casseroles and meals for me to store in the freezer, but this time, she was too busy. I have to say that I'm glad my wife will be here tomorrow. I'm tired of eating fast food."

Declan nodded in agreement. "Sherri throws down in the kitchen. And she loves to cook. I also have to add that Everleigh knows her way around the kitchen."

He enjoyed watching her interact with his nephew. Every time she laughed; the sound was like music to his ears.

Remy cleaned the kitchen after they finished eating.

"I'm glad you were able to get some rest earlier," Declan said.

"I didn't realize until we got here that I was so tired. Now that I'm thinking about it, I don't think I've slept really well since getting that letter."

"I want you to know that you and Rae are safe. No one knows where you are. You can relax."

"How about a quiet stroll around the lake? Rae can come with us."

Everleigh met his gaze, then said, "Sure. It's a nice evening for it."

They slipped on coats and went outside.

"I'm trying to convince myself that I'm on vacation in this beautiful house on the lake," Everleigh said as they walked the grounds.

He smiled. "That's a great way to look at it."

"Who knew that we'd be spending the holidays together," Everleigh murmured, pulling the folds of her coat together.

"I didn't, but I'm actually looking forward to getting to know you better."

"I am, too. I'd like to have a friend."

"So, *friend*...what do you like to do for fun?" Declan asked. He was glad to hear that she considered him a friend, but he also felt slightly dejected.

"Fun? What's that?" Everleigh chuckled. "Seriously, I love all things basketball..."

He looked surprised. "Wha-a-at?"

"Don't act like you haven't seen me and Rae at the games. We sit two rows behind you."

"I thought you were just coming to support the team."

"No, we love it," she responded. "I also enjoy reading, love going to the movies and trying new things."

"Have you ever gone on a sunset sail?"

"I haven't."

"Okay, that's something we can do while we're here. I'll take you on a tour around the lake," Declan said. "We can go tomorrow evening and take the girls. Rae and Halle will enjoy seeing all the Christmas decorations."

"Sounds like fun," Everleigh said. "I'm looking forward to that myself."

"Tell the truth...are you all hyped up for the holidays?"

She grinned. "I'm really grateful Rae and I don't have to spend it alone. I wasn't looking forward to that."

"Do you have any other family?" Declan inquired, then added, "On your mother's side."

"My mom was an only child. You met Bonnie—she was my mother's first cousin. I have distant cousins like her but they're spread out."

He took her hand in his. "I'm glad to have y'all here celebrating with us."

"'Jingle bells, jingle bells…'"

Declan and Everleigh stood there listening to Rae sing. The little girl stopped in her tracks and looked at them. "Sing!"

"'Jingle bells…'" they all sang as they strolled back to the house.

Despite being in South Carolina, Everleigh knew the nightmare was far from over.

"Having you and Remy here makes me feel safe," Everleigh said after she put Rae to bed and joined Declan in the family room. "I see he's following in your footsteps."

"He's always wanted to be in law enforcement. My sister works for Homeland Security."

"Oh, wow," she murmured, impressed.

"My grandfather was an attorney. My father was a prosecutor, then a judge. I guess the law in one form or another is in our blood."

"I would agree."

"Remy's wife, Sherri…she's in school to become a registered nurse."

"That's wonderful," Everleigh responded. "My mother was a nurse."

"Her mother is moving in with them to help with their daughter. She's a retired teacher and she'll be homeschooling Halle."

"That's really nice that Halle will be surrounded by both grandmothers."

"My brother-in-law lives nearby. He and my sister divorced a couple years ago, but I have a feeling that they're going to reconcile. They're the best of friends. He never got comfortable with her working in Homeland Security."

"How often do you get to see your parents?"

"Two or three times a year," Declan responded. "They decided to spend Christmas on a cruise this year."

"I think it's wonderful that you still have your parents."

"I realize this more and more each day."

"Declan, I have to say that it amazes me some woman hasn't snatched you up. You're a good man."

He laughed. "Maybe I still need to work out some soul issues—at least that's what I tell myself. I don't just want to get married. I want to spend the rest of my life with the *right* woman."

"I get that," Everleigh said.

She wondered what type of woman Declan would choose to marry, then pushed the thought out of her mind. She had no right to think along those lines. She'd dismissed the first kiss as nerves in a tense situation. The second kiss… Everleigh wasn't quite sure what to think. Was there something more between them? She forced the thought away. She needed to focus on keeping Rae safe.

"Do you think Neil will try to finish what his brother started?" Everleigh asked. She couldn't help her thoughts turning back to the present danger.

"It's possible," he responded.

"I sent you a copy of the camera footage of Ellis. I guess he wasn't worried about the cameras outside the house."

"He's going to jail for sure."

"I'm glad to hear that," Everleigh said, folding her arms across her chest. "It's what he deserves. Same as Powell. He should be punished for his crimes."

SIXTEEN

Everleigh woke to the smell of coffee floating down the hall from the kitchen. Declan must have come into the main house, she thought.

She took a deep breath before tossing back the covers and getting out of bed. She got dressed in a pair of jeans and a sweatshirt. Her hair flowed freely as she slipped on a pair of wool socks, then headed to the kitchen.

Steam wafted from the perking coffee maker with a pair of mugs waiting nearby. Her smile faded as she realized the machine was on auto.

Declan hadn't come down from the garage apartment yet. She didn't really like being in a stranger's house alone—it felt like she was invading the owner's privacy, even if it was with good reason.

Everleigh peered into the refrigerator.

"Mama…" Rae cried out when she walked into the kitchen. "I didn't know where you were."

She pulled her daughter into her arms. "I'd never leave without telling you, sweetie. And you know that I'd never leave you alone."

"Are you cooking breakfast?"

"I was thinking about it," Everleigh replied. "There's eggs, bacon, sausage…"

"Scrambled eggs, bacon…an-n-n-nd toast."

"Sounds good. I'll get right on it. You go brush your teeth and wash your face."

"Is Mr. Declan gonna eat with us?" Rae asked.

"I'm not sure," she responded. "I haven't talked to him yet."

"You should cook enough for him. He said he likes your cooking."

"Go brush your teeth, missy."

Laughing, Rae ran out of the kitchen.

Everleigh's gaze traveled the area. A shiny black-handled kettle in red sat on the stainless-steel stove. Black utensils were arranged in a red ceramic holder beside a matching set of canisters containing flour, sugar and coffee.

Near the window, wooden chairs were tucked neatly around a well-used granite-top table. In the center, a beautiful arrangement of silk roses in a red vase stood surrounded by miniature candles.

She could see a thin layer of dust on the window ledge.

Rae's return put an end to her musings.

Everleigh cooked bacon and scrambled eggs, as promised. She'd found a melon in the fridge and cut slices for her and Rae.

They sat down to eat as soon as the toast was ready.

"Are we gonna live here now?" Rae queried.

"No, we're not," she responded. "We're just staying here for a few days."

"Oh, it's a real nice house. How come we can't just let this be our new house? It has a huge playroom upstairs."

"Sweetie, this house belongs to Declan's sister. She's working out of town for a couple months. We're just here for the holidays."

Rae scooped up a forkful of eggs. "I hope we get to stay here for a long time."

Everleigh smiled. "You must really like it here."

"I do," she responded. "I like our house, too, Mama, even if this one is bigger."

"It's definitely larger than our home, but we don't really need anything this big. It's just you and me."

"Is Halle still coming today?"

"Yes. I know you can hardly wait to meet this little girl. I haven't seen you this excited in a long time."

"She gonna be my friend. Billie is coming, too."

"Really?"

Rae nodded. "Mr. Declan told me that she's coming with Halle." Taking Everleigh's hand in her small one, she continued, "Mama, I want a puppy."

"I know you do," she replied. Rae's opinion of dogs had changed drastically since she'd met Declan's Lab. "We need to get settled first, then we'll look for the perfect puppy for our home."

"Okay." Rae danced around the room.

Declan arrived halfway through the meal.

"You're just in time," Everleigh said. "There's more, but you'll have to heat it up."

"Not a problem. I'm starved."

"I feel terrible eating up your sister's food. I'm making a list so that I can replace what we've eaten."

"You don't have to worry about that," he responded. "I bought all this stuff and had it delivered here."

"Really?" Everleigh asked.

He smiled. "We have to eat."

"When is Halle coming?" Rae inquired.

"When I spoke to Remy, he said they were about an hour away."

The little girl's smile disappeared. "That's so long."

"She'll be here before you know it," he assured her.

Remy entered the kitchen. "I hope I didn't miss out on a hot breakfast. I'm tired of cereal."

"Help yourself," Everleigh said.

"Is Halle almost here?" Rae asked after they were finished with breakfast.

Remy grinned. "They should be arriving soon. She's excited about meeting you."

Everleigh's gaze drifted out the window. After a few moments, Declan touched her elbow.

"What are you thinking about?" he asked.

"I was thinking about Ellis and Neil," she responded. "I was angry initially, but the more I think about them... I feel bad."

He wore a look of confusion on his face. "Why?"

"Because I understand the root cause. Grief and anger. Their anger stems from a situation in which they tragically lost their mother. They can't strike out at James Ray Powell, so they're coming after his family...coming after me. They don't realize that it's not going to bring them the results they desire, though."

"You're amazing, Everleigh. Ellis wanted to harm you and Rae. Yet, you're still compassionate toward him and his brother."

"No, I'm not. I just understand their reasons. I do pray for God to soften their hearts. Maybe Neil will leave us alone now that Ellis is in jail."

"I'll feel better when he's behind bars as well," Declan said.

"He's probably gone into hiding."

"Maybe, but at some point, he will be found."

"I hope so," Everleigh said.

She and Rae were taking a stroll around the lake when a car pulled up to the guesthouse.

"Mama, is that them?"

"I think so," Everleigh answered.

As soon as the door to the SUV opened, Billie rushed out as if happy to experience freedom.

Rae squealed with delight when the dog bounded for them.

A little girl with two fluffy ponytails came running behind her. "Billie... Billie..."

"It's *Halle*," her daughter said and took off running toward her.

She prayed Rae didn't scare the little girl off.

Everleigh's eyes filled with water at the sight of the two little girls hugging each other as if they were lifelong friends. Billie licked at their heels, wanting to get in on the action.

Declan walked out of garage and joined her. "Just looking at them, you wouldn't think Halle and Rae are just meeting for the first time."

She smiled. "I was just thinking that same thing. I think it's so beautiful."

They were joined by Remy and Sherri, and Declan made the introductions.

"Your little girl is so adorable," Sherri said. "She was grinning ear to ear when she ran up to Halle. Then she just hugged her."

"I was a bit worried she'd scare little Halle," Everleigh responded with a chuckle.

"Oh, no. Remy had already told her about Rae. She was just as excited about having someone to play with."

"Everleigh and I will keep an eye on the girls," Declan said. "I'm sure you and Sherri want to get the SUV unpacked."

"Thank you," Sherri responded. "It shouldn't take long."

Declan winked at his nephew. "No need to rush."

Grinning, Everleigh said, "I've learned something else about you."

"What's that?"

"You're a romantic. That was incredibly sweet of you to give them some time alone."

"I hope you don't mind that I recruited you to help me watch Halle."

"Not at all," she responded. "I think we should get them in the house. I can make lunch." She pointed toward the dock. "The boat out there...does it belong to your sister?"

"Actually, it's mine," Declan revealed.

"It's nice."

"That's the one we'll use for the sunset sail, if you're still interested. We can take the boat out this evening. People come from all over to see these houses decorated for Christmas."

"Sounds like fun. I can't wait."

Everleigh felt safe and secure, but she couldn't forget that this was temporary. After the holidays, she and Rae would be returning home. If Neil was still running free...

She shook away the thought. She wasn't going to worry about this now.

After dinner, Declan helped Halle and Rae into the boat after ensuring both girls were in life jackets.

Everleigh sat on the hard plastic seat wearing one as well.

He took his time motoring them around the lake.

"O-o-oh," Rae uttered. "Mama...the lights are so pretty."

"Yes, they are."

"Every house on the lake decorates for the holidays," Declan said.

"It's looks almost magical," Everleigh said.

When they returned, Declan secured the boat to the dock. Remy and Sherri were waiting for them on the dock. He helped the girls out first then assisted Everleigh.

"Sherri made hot chocolate and gingerbread cookies for y'all."

"Yay," Rae said.

Halle followed suit.

"Did you enjoy yourself?" Declan inquired.

"I did," Everleigh responded. "It's been a long time since I was on a boat. This was nice."

"Maybe you and Rae will come back when it's warmer—that's when I spend most of my time going up and down this lake."

"Sounds like fun."

"This is the way I like seeing you," he said. "You look really relaxed right now."

"Probably because I feel safe here."

Her words brought a smile to his lips. "That was the goal."

He placed an arm around Everleigh, wanting her to feel as if she was wrapped in an invisible warmth. He looked over at her, trying to assess her unreadable features.

She turned to face him. "What are you thinking about right now?" she asked.

Declan slowly looked down at her, his stomach dropping like a book tumbling off the top shelf as his gaze meshed with hers. Where their fingers touched, he felt a gentle warmth right to his core.

When Declan and Remy finished, the exterior windows were bejeweled with sparkling lights that glittered brightly.

"You and Remy did a great job," Everleigh said.

"We found some red and gold tinsel in a box in the garage," Declan responded. "There was a crate filled with ornaments right beside it. All we have to do is pick out a Christmas tree."

"When are you doing that?"

"Remy and Sherri are going this afternoon and they're taking Halle. I think Rae should go with them if that's okay with you."

"It's fine," she responded.

They left an hour later.

"I need to take care of some paperwork but it shouldn't take too long."

"It's fine. I need to get some air," Everleigh stated abruptly. She was beginning to feel like she couldn't breathe. She felt trapped.

"I'll go with you. I can—"

Shaking her head, she said, "If you don't mind… I just need some time alone, Declan."

He gave a slight nod. "Okay, but try to stay on this side of the lake."

Outside, she walked the trail, hoping the fresh air would help unsettle her troubled mind.

"Evvie…"

The hair on the back of her neck stood up. Everleigh turned around to face Wyle Gaines. "You don't have the right to call me that." She wasn't intimidated by his height towering over her. He kept his hands in the pockets of his dark sweatpants.

Staring her down, he responded, "Still so high and mighty."

"How did you find me?"

"I put a GPS tracker on your friend's car," he said with a nonchalant shrug. "There are some dangerous people after you. I guess you've figured that out already."

"You clearly couldn't keep your big mouth shut," Everleigh said. "I can't believe my mother trusted you with her secret."

"She didn't," Wyle answered. "Deloris never would've

told me about your father. I could never get her to tell me anything about him."

Confusion colored Everleigh's expression. "Then how did you find out?"

"I overheard Deloris telling *you* that James Ray Powell was your father. After you refused to sell me the house… I got drunk at this bar and I guess I said too much. Those brothers…dangerous bunch. They bought me drink after drink and kept asking me about Deloris. I told them she'd died, then I told them about you."

"You're a horrible man."

"If I was really horrible, I'd tell them where you are. They asked me to find you."

"So they know I'm here in Columbia?" Everleigh asked, not quite sure if she could believe Wyle.

"No, and they won't know… I just need you to do something for me."

Folding her arms across her chest, she asked, "What? Sell you my mother's house?" Everleigh hoped Declan would soon come looking for her.

"I'm thinking more like you sign it over to me. Your life and Rae's…that's worth much more than a little property, don't you think?"

"You're really a piece of work, Wyle." She didn't bother to hide her contempt. "I don't know how you were able to fool my mom, but I know you're nothing but a fraud."

"I can always hand you over to the brothers personally."

Wyle was talking as if he didn't know Ellis had been arrested. Everleigh decided not to mention it to him, either.

"I'd like to see you try that," she uttered, moving slowly toward him, hands balled into fists.

"Just give me the house and you'll never hear from me again."

"No."

Anger flashed in his hazel eyes. "These men won't hesitate to kill you. They are all filled with pure hate. I've seen it in them."

"So, you know they're murderers, huh?"

He seemed confused by her question. "Huh? No. But they're violent. And they threatened to come after me if I didn't give them you."

Everleigh glimpsed Declan easing up behind Wyle, his hand on his gun.

"In case you don't know, the police are looking for you."

"Why? I haven't broken any laws," he snapped. "What did you tell them?"

"You hacked into my alarm system and broke into my house, Wyle."

"Look…" He looked as if he was about to take a step toward her. "You're not about to set me up. All I did was disable the alarm. Ellis made me do it. Evvie, I came here because I don't want to see any harm come to you and Rae. But I'm telling you…those dudes are cr—"

"Don't move," Declan ordered. "Put your hands on your head."

"You don't know what you're doing," Wyle said. "Everleigh, I can help you."

"No thanks," she responded.

Declan handcuffed him as sirens began to sound in the distance.

"Check your car," she said. "Wyle put a tracker on it."

The local police arrived.

"I'm the only one who can save you from the brothers," he said as they escorted him to the cruiser.

Everleigh embraced Declan. "He wanted me to sign my mom's house over to him in exchange for my life and Rae's."

"It wouldn't have stopped anything. Neil would still come

after you," he said, "but he'd have the property free and clear."

"I was thinking the same thing."

"I'm going down to the precinct. Stay in the house. Remy should be back soon."

Everleigh nodded, rubbing her arms. "I'm going to make some tea to help steady my nerves."

"Maybe I shouldn't leave right now. If Wyle was able to track us…maybe he already told Neil how to find you."

"Wyle said he wouldn't give them my location if I signed over the house to him. That was the offer he made me. You go and I'll be fine. I think he was telling the truth about that."

Remy's SUV pulled into the driveway.

"Good, they're back," Declan said.

They had come home with a tall, full live tree.

"I can't wait to decorate it," Rae said when they entered the house. "I like doing that. Me and Daddy used to decorate the tree while Mama baked cookies."

It made her feel good to see her daughter like this and know that she had good memories of Britt. Everleigh wasn't sure how resilient and well-adjusted Rae was after the loss of both her father and grandmother.

"Where did Mr. Declan go?"

"He had to run an errand," Everleigh answered. "He shouldn't be gone too long." Once again, she was grateful that Rae—and Halle—hadn't been around to see Wyle taken into custody.

When Declan returned, he complimented the girls and Sherri on the tree decorations.

"The Christmas tree was Rae and Britt's thing," Everleigh said. "We didn't have a tree last year."

"It will get easier with time," he responded. "Give yourself some grace."

"Some days I feel a bit overwhelmed."

"I think anyone would feel the same way in your shoes."

"But when I look at Rae, she just makes everything so much better for me. I'm not making any sense, am I?"

"You're making a lot of sense," he responded. "Children like Rae and Halle restore my hope for the future."

SEVENTEEN

Declan watched his nephew with Sherri and Halle and felt a thread of envy.

He yearned for a wife and family. It came as a bit of a surprise to him, because Declan hadn't thought much about it in recent years. He long accepted the fact that maybe he was destined to remain single. He had even found a measure of contentment in his bachelor lifestyle even though it wasn't his personal choice.

Spending the past few weeks with Everleigh and Rae brought those desires back to the surface. He wanted nothing more than to see them safe. It didn't seem fair that they had been targeted by two men hungry for vengeance and another out of pure greed. He took consolation that even in this situation, God was able to turn it into a blessing.

Everleigh was quiet through most of the evening. She chatted with Sherri and Remy, but other than that, she didn't say much until after everyone else had gone to bed.

"Declan, I don't know what I would've done without you today. Wyle was determined to force me to give him the property. Before I didn't really think he'd resort to violence…now I'm not so sure."

Her hand felt like silk in his. As he met Everleigh's warm gaze, affection for her jerked at his heart. Declan quickly pushed away his emotions. This wasn't the time or place to dwell on his feelings.

"I wasn't about to let anything happen." Declan reluctantly pulled away, then stood up and stretched. "I feel like some hot chocolate. What about you?"

"Sure," Everleigh replied smoothly.

He walked the short distance to the kitchen.

When he returned with two steaming mugs, Declan found her sleeping. She'd curled into a ball on the floor, a throw pillow cushioning her head.

He sat down and listened until Everleigh's breathing became steady and deep. She looked peaceful as she slept. Declan reached into a nearby basket and retrieved another blanket, placing it over his legs. He leaned back, using the couch as a backrest.

He'd been surprised by his reaction to her touch when she grabbed his hand. There had been times during his career when female victims grew attached to him. Often, they wanted to build something more, but he knew that most relationships born out of trauma failed.

The best thing for Declan was to keep things professional with Everleigh. Besides, she was still grieving the loss of her husband. His eyes strayed to the wedding rings on her left hand.

He turned his attention to the movie he and Everleigh had been waiting to come on. Declan didn't bother to wake her.

Fifteen minutes into the movie, he felt himself begin to nod off. Declan jerked awake. He was determined to watch until the end.

"Is today Christmas?" Rae asked.

"It's tomorrow, sweetie."

"Yay," Halle and Rae said in unison.

Everleigh broke into a smile. "Sherri, I'm so glad Halle is here. She's been able to keep my daughter entertained."

"I feel the same way about Rae," she responded. "Halle loves her grandparents, but she doesn't have anyone to play with whenever we're here."

"Declan tells me that you'll be living here soon."

Sherri nodded. "As soon as I graduate. It's been hard being away from Remy. When he applied to the police department here, we thought it would take a while. The process moved much quicker than we anticipated."

"I'd love to schedule some playdates if you and Remy ever come to Charleston."

"Of course. Remy and Declan are very close and they enjoy hanging out together. While they're out doing their thing, we can do something with the girls. And if you're interested...maybe squeeze in a girl's day or night out for us."

"I'd love that," Everleigh responded.

"Remy and Declan are going to take the girls to lunch and to do some Christmas shopping. While they're out, we can run some errands. I need to pick up some items for dinner tomorrow."

"Sherri, what can I do to help? I can cook for tonight and I'm happy to help with the Christmas meal. I make a pretty good macaroni and cheese, candied yams and dressing."

"Sounds good to me," she responded. "I'll focus on the chicken, mixed greens and sweet-potato pies. Declan always smokes the turkey and salmon. Remy...my poor hubby is in charge of putting the ice in the glasses and setting the table."

Everleigh laughed. "He said cooking wasn't his gift."

Laughing, Sherri said, "He was telling the whole truth of that. That man can barely boil a pot of water."

She enjoyed spending her afternoon with Sherri. They

picked up some last-minutes gifts, then had a nice lunch at one of the restaurants in downtown Columbia. She was grateful not to have to constantly look over her shoulder.

"I'm glad you suggested we get these wrapped before going back to the house," Everleigh stated. "I don't know how I'd be able to get them past Rae. Oh, and thanks for the suggestion on what to get Declan." She'd wanted to have something under the tree for him, but was at a loss as to what would be appropriate.

"He's gonna love that wireless charging mat," Sherri said. "He's been wanting one since he saw mine."

Back at the house, Everleigh put her packages in the bedroom, then headed to the kitchen to prepare dinner.

"I'm surprised Declan and Remy aren't back with the girls," Sherry said when she joined her.

"Declan just texted me. They took them to a festival for an hour, but are heading home now."

"They probably wanted to tire them out so they'd go to bed early."

Everleigh chuckled. "Rae's so excited about Christmas... I'm going to have a hard time getting her to go to sleep tonight."

"Halle will try to hang on, but one thing about her— when she's tired, she will go to bed."

"How long have you known Declan?"

"Not very long," she responded. "I started teaching in August. I met him that first week at a faculty meeting."

"He's a really nice man, Everleigh."

"Yes, he is," she said. "It surprises me he's still single."

"Declan's very particular," Sherri responded. "As he should be."

"I agree."

"He mentioned that your husband passed away. I'm very sorry for your loss. I can't imagine..."

"I wouldn't wish that on anybody, Sherri. My husband was wonderful—and a great father. We just lost him much too soon."

"I see you still wear your wedding rings."

"I've thought about taking them off but... I'm not ready."

"Take as much time as you need, Everleigh. There isn't a set time limit when it comes to grief. It's different for everyone."

"A lot of people don't understand that."

"I lost my father three years ago," Sherri said. "I still grieve. My mother remarried last year and I was really upset with her at first. She explained to me that she and my dad truly loved each other—they had a loving and fulfilling marriage. She said that while she would never forget him, she was a woman who loved being married. She didn't just want companionship—she wanted a husband. She said she could move on without regrets or guilt because she'd been a good and faithful wife to my dad."

"How did you feel after that conversation?"

"Better. Much better. My mom is very happy. She would tell that she's been doubly blessed to have found love with two wonderful men in her lifetime."

Everleigh smiled. "I would have to agree with your mother. It is indeed a blessing."

"We're back," Declan said when he entered the house.

"Mama, I got you a present," Rae said, rushing into the kitchen. "I'ma put it under the tree after I wrap it."

"Thank you, sweetie," Everleigh replied as she leaned down to plant a kiss on her daughter's forehead.

Remy kissed his wife, then said, "We're taking the girls to the guesthouse so they can wrap their gifts."

"Dinner will be ready in about forty-five minutes," Everleigh announced.

"Don't worry," Declan responded. "We're not going to miss that."

Everleigh returned her attention to preparing dinner. She made meatballs from the ground-beef mixture. "Spaghetti is the perfect choice for tonight since we're having a feast tomorrow."

"Yeah, I figured we'd keep it simple. Besides, they all *love* spaghetti and meatballs."

"What's not to love?" she asked with a chuckle. "Rae and I can eat it all week long. We don't, but we could."

"We're the same way," Sherri stated while making a dinner salad. "Pasta is a staple in our house, too."

Sure enough, when Rae sat down at the dining room table, she exclaimed, "Spaghetti and meatballs...yay!"

"I love sp'ghetti," Halle agreed.

Everleigh listened to Rae and Declan interacting over their meal. Hearing them talk and laugh, she realized that he was bonding with her daughter in a special way. He would be a wonderful father one day, she thought to herself.

After her husband died, she'd put all her energy into her job and her daughter. There had been men who expressed interest in her, but she wasn't ready. Then her mother's cancer diagnosis came—Everleigh had no time for anything else outside her family.

Her hand curled into a fist under the table. Though she felt a growing affection for Declan, she didn't think she had the emotional capacity to open herself to heartache again. Losing Britt had almost killed her. It wasn't something she wanted to go through ever again.

Everleigh told herself that once the threat was over, she and Declan would remain friends. Nothing more. However, this declaration seemed to bring with it a certain sadness.

She decided not to ponder on it any further. Instead, she opted to enjoy the food and the fellowship.

Sherri brought out dessert.

"My baby knows what I like," Remy declared with a grin. "She made her famous peppermint chocolate cake."

"I want cake," Rae said.

"Finish up your spaghetti first," Everleigh responded. "Then you can have dessert."

She bit back her laughter when Rae stuffed her mouth with a meatball.

"Finish up, but slow down, sweetie. The cake isn't going anywhere."

"I'll cut you a slice of it and put it aside until you're done," Declan said, picking up a small plate.

After swallowing, Rae responded, "Thank you, Mr. Declan."

When he cut a huge slice for himself, Everleigh asked, "Can I have a bite of yours? I don't want to overindulge."

"Sure."

Rae clapped her hands, then said, "Mr. Declan loves Mama."

Everleigh's fork fell to her plate. "Sweetie...we're *friends*. You shouldn't go around saying something like that."

She stole a peek at Declan, who looked like he'd been shocked speechless.

"But, Mama, you said that if a man shares his cake with you, he loves you."

"My mother told me the same thing," Sherri said. "Just saying…"

"Rae, I care about your mom and about you," Declan stated. "Friends can also share cake, too."

"I'm your friend," she responded. "So you have to share with me, too. You can't eat it all."

Remy burst into laughter. "Uncle, please tell me you saw that coming. She has her slice and some of yours, too."

Laughter rang out around the table.

Everleigh sent Remy a grateful smile for changing the flow of the conversation. When she glanced at Declan, he looked amused. He didn't look at all uncomfortable, which helped to ease her own stress.

Going forward, she would have to be careful with what she said around Rae, Everleigh decided. Her daughter was like a sponge, soaking up everything.

"Why don't you guys just stay here in the main house tonight," Declan suggested when they moved to the family room after dinner. "We can bring Christmas in together."

Sherri looked at Everleigh, then said, "I told you we should have gotten those pajamas…"

He glanced over at her. "You didn't want to do the whole matching-PJs thing? I thought you had real Christmas spirit."

"I didn't mind it—I wasn't sure how you or Remy might feel about it."

"Sherri knows I'm always down for the family."

"Rae and I…"

"Are still family," Remy said. "At least for the holidays."

Declan agreed. "Whenever you're with us, you become family."

Smiling, Everleigh responded, "I've learned something new about you."

"What's that?"

"You bring home strays. I bet you've always done that."

"She knows you, Declan," his nephew stated. "My mom used to get so mad with him when they were growing up. He was always bringing home animals. He didn't care what it was—dog, cat, bird… He even brought home a snake one time."

"That didn't go over well at all," Declan responded with a chuckle. "My sister was okay if it was a dog. Anything else had to go. She'd go running to our parents complaining."

"I can't say I wouldn't have done the same," Everleigh replied.

"Snakes are scary," Rae interjected. "I don't like snakes."

"Me, either," Sherri said.

"Okay…okay. I get it. I won't be picking up any stray snakes while we're here."

A collective sigh floated across the air.

Shortly after ten, Remy carried a sleeping Halle upstairs to bed.

"Mama, I'm getting tired, too."

Standing, Everleigh said, "I guess that's my cue. Rae and I are going to call it a night. We'll see y'all in the morning."

Declan eyed her. "G'night."

Everleigh took Rae to the bedroom.

"I'm gonna take this time to get some of the cooking out of the way," Sherri stated.

Remy looked over at Declan and said, "Uncle, you should've seen the look on your face earlier. You looked like you'd been caught with your hand in the cookie jar."

He laughed. "I froze. I didn't really know how to respond."

"Especially since you haven't fully accepted the truth of it yourself."

There was no point in lying, so Declan simply shrugged.

"Did you get any information out of Wyle Gaines?" Remy asked.

"He said that he'd promised Everleigh's mother that he

would look out for her and Rae. Said that's all he was trying to do before he lawyered up."

"So he's actually denying everything he said to Everleigh?"

Declan nodded. "Said he didn't have any idea what she
was talking about. Wyle even claimed that Everleigh's
angry because he rebuffed her advances."

"Did you tell her any of this?"

"No, I didn't want to upset her. Besides, I'd take her
word over Wyle's any day of the week."

"What *did* you tell Everleigh?" Remy inquired.

"Just that he lawyered up," Declan responded. "When
I asked him about the tracker, he didn't confirm or deny.
I thought for a minute Wyle was going to say that she put
it on the car, but apparently, he thought better of it."

"What's his connection to the Ragland brothers?"

"Wyle told Everleigh that she met them in a bar. He had
been drinking and was talking to anyone who'd listen that
she was evil, like her serial-killer daddy. They became
friendly with him and coaxed him to tell them more."

"I'm sure you asked Wyle for the missing brother's location."

"I did. He said he didn't know. That he hadn't talked to
them since that night."

"Do you believe him?"

Declan rubbed his chin. "I'm not sure. I don't see them
trusting a man like Wyle."

Remy nodded in agreement. "He sounds like a loose
cannon."

"I was hoping to get a lead on Neil. He could be anywhere. I even considered that maybe they have been keeping tabs on Wyle. Maybe even followed him here." He
looked into the blazing fire as flames licked at the wood.
"I know she's ready for this to be over."

"It would've been a nice Christmas present," Remy said.

"I was thinking the same thing."

"At least you have Wyle and Ellis. Soon you'll have Neil in custody, too. You know I'll do what I can to help you with this, Uncle. I checked the camera footage and Wyle is the only person who set foot on the property."

"Neil will make a move—he has to."

"I agree, Remy. We just don't know when or where."

EIGHTEEN

Everleigh took in a deep breath.

Her stomach tightened as the memories of life with Britt washed over her. Sitting so close to Declan was having an effect on her. His body heat encircled her, making her dizzy. She'd felt a spark of something when he'd held her hand, too.

The attraction was not unexpected. Everleigh knew it was normal for an individual to be drawn to her protector, often after being thrown together through traumatic events or responding out of need. She'd seen this in the behavior of a few former clients. Still, Everleigh struggled in gauging her own feelings. She considered that possibly there was something more going on between them, but it was a passing thought. Not one she wanted to contemplate at the moment. She had more pressing matters to contend with.

Unable to sleep, she shifted her position in bed, turning to her left side.

It would be unfair to Declan to pursue a relationship she wasn't ready for. Everleigh didn't want to risk hurting him. He didn't deserve that. She also had to think of Rae and her attachment to Declan. She affirmed once more that it was best that they keep their relationship platonic.

The thought of Declan finding love with another woman didn't sit well with Everleigh, however.

I can't have it both ways.

The truth was that she didn't want to spend the rest of her life a widow. Everleigh could admit that she wanted to be married again; she wanted more children, too. *Give me the strength and the courage to move past my grief and my guilt,* she prayed. Everleigh didn't want to keep feeling as if she were betraying her husband with her feelings for Declan. Especially when she knew Britt didn't want her to stop living—he'd told her as much. He once told her that he hoped she'd find love and remarry quickly because he didn't want Everleigh and Rae to be alone. It was almost as if he'd known he would die a year later.

Rae woke up shortly after 6:00 a.m. "Merry Christmas, Mama."

"What are you doing up so early? I can barely wake you when you have to go to school."

"Can we get up now and open presents?"

"We're going to open gifts after everybody is up."

"That's gonna take a long time," Rae pouted.

"Maybe not." Everleigh slid out of bed. "C'mon, let's go wash our faces and brush our teeth. I'll check to see if anybody is up."

"They don't wanna sleep Christmas away," Rae said.

"I'm sure they don't, sweetie. I'll be back shortly."

The scent from the Christmas tree was strong, beckoning her into the family room. The sun sparkled bright through the huge windows, making the ornaments glisten. Holiday music suddenly poured out through the speakers embedded in the wall.

A smile trembled on her lips as Everleigh turned around.

"Merry Christmas." Declan stood there wearing a Santa hat with his arms filled with stockings. "I meant to hang these up last night but fell asleep."

"Let's do it now," she said, crossing the floor to relieve him of a couple.

They hung them across the fireplace. Billie ambled over to the tree and began sniffing at the wrapped gifts beneath.

They were soon joined by Remy.

"Merry Christmas, fam," he said. "Everything ready for the girls?"

"I believe so," Everleigh responded.

"Let the festivities began," Declan said. "I need to get my camera. It's in the apartment. Nobody touch a present until I get back."

"It's obvious he don't have children. They don't care about pictures."

Everleigh chuckled. "I guess I'll go get Rae. She's been up for almost an hour and I wouldn't let her leave the bedroom."

"Sherri and Halle should be down any minute."

Declan was back when she returned with Rae. The little girl ran over to Billie. "Merry Christmas, girl. I have a present for you."

"Marry Chrissmas," Halle said when she ran into the room. She embraced Rae and Billie. Not to be outdone, Billie licked them both.

"Billie! Stop that," Declan said. "She's just as excited as the girls."

"You should get a photo of the three of them," Everleigh suggested.

Sherri agreed.

They sat down to watch the girls open their gifts while Declan documented the day with his camera.

Everleigh blinked back tears of happiness. It was a delight to see Rae laughing and smiling after so much sadness. That first Christmas after Britt died, they had dinner with her mother, but the presents went unopened for two days. She and Rae were both in the thick of their grief, and her mother was sick. Everleigh was determined this year would be different.

When she'd woken up earlier, she'd felt a sadness because Deloris wasn't with them, but Rae cheered her up when she said, "Daddy and Grandma are having the best Christmas because they live in heaven now."

Everleigh carried the sentiment in her heart and it gave her joy. Deloris wasn't sick anymore and she was with family. In her mind, she could see her mother and husband together, their faces filled with smiles—smiles that radiated down to her.

Sherri sat down beside her. "Everleigh, I have to tell you how much I admire you. It takes a pretty strong woman to take care of a terminally ill mother in the midst of grieving the loss of your husband. Then moving to a new city and starting over. You're amazing."

"Thank you for saying that, Sherri. I have to confess I don't always feel so strong. In fact, there have been times when I've felt completely helpless. But then God brought Declan into my life."

"And now you have Remy and me. We've adopted you and Rae into our family. The girls get along so well, one would think they've known each other forever." Smiling, she added, "I feel the same way about you."

The two women embraced.

"I'm really glad to see Rae having such a good time. I think she needed this."

"How are you doing, really?"

"I'm fine until I think of having to go back home. Then I start to imagine the worst. But I rein in my thoughts." Her stomach knotted up and a sense of dread crept up her spine at the thought that Neil was somewhere out there.

"Declan is very good at his job and I know he'll find that guy."

"I trust him," she responded with a smile.

Billie trotted over, her toenails clicking on the hardwood, and prodded her furry head under Everleigh's hand, whining faintly. Automatically, she tugged the dog against her leg, rubbing her back. "Merry Christmas to you, too."

NINETEEN

"Sherri, you and Everleigh outdid yourselves in the kitchen. Dinner was fantastic," Declan said, rubbing his belly. "Now if you'll roll yourself into the family room, Remy and I will clean up."

"I don't mind helping," Everleigh said.

"You've done enough," Remy stated. "You two get a pass this year. Next year, y'all are in charge of clean-up."

She glanced at Declan, who stated, "I guess that means you and Rae have to join us next Christmas. I'm not doing it alone."

Tears welled in her eyes. Everleigh wiped them away. "I've been trying to hold them in all day. I am awestruck by the kindness and generosity shown to Rae and me. I was feeling so alone in the world after losing Britt and my mother." Her voice broke. "M-my heart rejoices because I see that God answered my prayers."

Declan took her hand in his own. "You and Rae mean a lot to me. You're not alone. When Wyle and the Ragland brothers are no longer a concern, I will still be around. Billie, too."

"I know that now."

He loved her—Declan knew this as sure as his own name. His feelings for any of the women in his past paled in comparison.

Everleigh turned and looked at him.

She held her arms out, low, palms facing him.

He blinked a couple times. Was she really offering him an embrace?

Declan didn't keep her waiting. He hugged her.

"There's so much I want to say to you," he whispered. "But now isn't the right time or place."

Everleigh gave a gentle nod.

His heart leaped with joy. This was the sign he'd been waiting for. Declan was more determined than ever to find Neil and put him in jail with his brother.

Everleigh snuggled under the blanket in front of the fireplace with Billie napping at her feet. Declan sat across from her with the girls. They had wrangled him into reading them a story.

Every now and then his eyes would venture to hers and he'd give her a secret smile, one filled with promise. Beneath the throw, Everleigh twisted the rings on her finger nervously. She'd almost taken them off earlier, but couldn't go through with it.

She told herself that she shouldn't rush this process. Everleigh was ready to move on, but she felt guilty for feeling this way. She considered the advice she'd give if a client came to her.

I'd tell the person that there isn't a time limit on grief, or when someone is ready for a new relationship. Some people are ready months after the death of their spouse, and for others, it may take years. Have I somehow placed an unrealistic expectation on myself of how long I should grieve?

Everleigh removed the rings and slipped them into the pocket of her jeans. There weren't any feelings of guilt, only peace.

Declan invited her to take a walk around the lake when the girls and Billie went upstairs to the playroom.

"It's so nice out here," Everleigh said. "The weather is perfect. Not too cold and not too hot. What's your favorite memory growing up here?"

"I'd have to say this Christmas," Declan responded. "Rae and Halle embody what it's like to see the world through the eyes of a child. In the job I do, I see a lot of the bad stuff going on in the world. Those two beautiful little girls have shown me the world in a different light. And then there's you, Everleigh. Just your presence has made this holiday special for me. I was given a preview of what life looks like when you've found the person who is a perfect fit for you." He met her gaze. "Do you understand what I'm trying to say?"

"I do," Everleigh responded. "And I feel the same way." She held up her left hand. "I'm ready to live again. I didn't really realize that I'd stopped living until the Ragland's forced their way into my life."

"I go back to work on New Year's Eve," Declan announced. "I'm putting all my focus on finding Neil Ragland. I'll come back to get you and Rae on the third."

They walked around the lake hand in hand as they laughed and talked. She and Declan paused to admire a huge oak tree.

"I love everything about this place," she said.

"Where we're standing right now is the land my parents gave to me. It's three acres. I've always planned to build a house here whenever I had a family. It's the perfect place to raise children."

"You're right," Everleigh said. "This place is perfect for a family."

Declan was tempted to say more, but instead asked, "Do you fish?"

Her smile disappeared. "Nope."

He gave a short laugh. "That's fine. Neither do I. We'll leave that to my sister."

Everleigh looped her arm through his. "Sounds great to me."

During their walk back to the house, she said, "I think we should set a trap for Neil."

"In what way?"

"He's probably been watching my house. I can go home and—"

Declan cut her off. "That's absolutely out of the question."

"Why? When I'm home, the island police will be close by. I'll be prepared."

"I won't have you putting yourself at risk. You have Rae to think about."

"As long as I'm away, Neil has no reason to make a move," Everleigh said. "We have to do something to draw him out."

"At some point he'll get impatient. He'll try to find a way to force you out of hiding."

"The only way I can imagine him doing that is if he came after Rae," she uttered. "I can't let that happen, Declan. We need to get to him first."

The days were flying by relentlessly. Already, it was the third day of the new year and soon enough, it would be gone. Everleigh remarked, "I wish Declan had been able to stay for New Year's."

"Me, too," Sherri said. "You two have gotten extremely close since Christmas, I see." She pointed to Everleigh's left hand. She was no longer wearing her rings.

"We have," she admitted. "But we're taking it really slow.

I can't fully focus on anything else other than the safety of my child at the moment."

"I know all of this is going to work out," Sherri said. "No harm will come to you and Rae. God will protect you."

"I do believe that," Everleigh responded.

Rae walked out of the bedroom wearing a pair of jeans and her cowboy boots.

"Where's your coat?"

"Oh, I forgot." She ran back to the bedroom, returning minutes later with a dark brown coat.

Halle walked into the house with Remy.

"Did you find her boots?" Sherri asked.

"I did," he answered. "They were under her bed."

Picking up her purse, Sherri said, "I guess we're ready to go."

During the short drive to the restaurant, Everleigh recalled a conversation with Deloris a few days before she died.

Evvie, you weren't made to live alone, without being surrounded by family. Having the same blood don't make you related. You have to open your heart... Sure, the stakes are higher, but it's worth it in the end.

Everleigh thought it was a strange thing for Deloris to say at the time. But now it made sense to her.

An image of Declan formed in her mind.

He was definitely worth the risk, she thought as a smile danced on her lips.

TWENTY

Declan drove to the university to pick up a textbook he'd left in his office.

When he left the building, there was a flurry of commotion around him, which prompted him to stop a security guard. "Hey, what's going on? Did something happen?"

"There's a gunman in the library. I heard there are five or six students inside."

"Are you sure about this?" Declan asked. "Did you get a look at the assailant?"

"He was tall—athletic build and long locks... He asked me for directions. He stuttered some. I never saw him before but I thought he was a student."

Neil Ragland.

Declan hated to call Everleigh with this news, but it would be better coming from him. Pretty soon, the campus would have media and police officers crawling all over it. While waiting for her to answer, an alert came across his phone. Everleigh would be receiving the same message.

As soon as she answered her phone, he said, "I wanted you to hear this from me. Neil's here on campus. He's in the library."

"I just got an alert about a gunman," Everleigh responded. "Do you know for sure that it's Neil?"

"According to the description I received from a security officer…it's him." Before she could reply, Declan said, "I have to go. I'll call you back."

He rushed over to where a crowd was slowly forming.

Thank God, most of the students were away for the holidays, he thought to himself. Declan was also relieved that Everleigh wasn't anywhere near the campus. At least she and Rae were safe.

"I need to get to the university," Everleigh told Sherri and Remy.

"We're two hours away."

"Then I need to leave right now. It's me he wants. I might be able to convince Neil to surrender." She looked at Sherri. "Are you fine with watching Rae while I'm gone?"

"Of course," she responded. "She'll stay in the guesthouse with us, but are you sure about this?"

"Declan will have a fit if I just let you go," Remy said. "Everleigh, you're putting yourself in danger."

"I want to make sure Neil doesn't hurt more innocent people, Remy."

"It's almost four. There's a flight leaving at five o'clock to Charleston. You'll get there much quicker. If you're ready, I can take you to the airport."

"Yes, I'm ready to leave. Remy, thank you," she responded. "And don't worry, I'll take care of your uncle."

Thirty minutes later, Everleigh was on the plane. She normally didn't like small planes but she didn't have any other choice.

It's time to put an end to this nightmare.

She prayed during the short flight to Charleston. Everleigh had texted Declan to let him know she was on her way to Charleston because she had to talk to Neil, try to reason with him.

Everleigh took an Uber to the university from the airport.

Faculty, staff and students had all undergone safety training for active-shooter and hostage situations. As soon as she arrived on campus, she saw that police officers surrounded the area.

She was approached by an officer.

"I work here," Everleigh said, showing her credentials. "Neil Ragland will want to speak with me."

She was led over to Declan.

"I wish you'd stayed in Columbia." he said when she joined them.

"I'm hoping I can talk Neil down. At least let me try."

"I'm not letting you go inside that library."

"We have to get those students out safely, Declan. Let me try to talk to him first."

He walked her over to the commander in charge. "This is Everleigh Taylor. She's the person he's after."

"I'd like to try to talk to Neil."

She whispered a silent prayer before picking up the phone.

"What?"

"Neil," Everleigh said calmly. "Please don't hurt the people inside. They don't have anything to do with this. I'm the person you want."

"Come join th-the p-party."

"Why don't you let the students leave first," she responded, ignoring the way Declan furiously shook his head.

"Neil, I understand the pain you're feeling."

"Your f-father is the c-cause of my pain."

"My mother was a victim, too. That's why she moved out of the apartment on Beech. She didn't know who he was at the time. My mother had no way of knowing that he would return and attack anyone else."

"Why did she l-leave then? She must've known he'd be back."

"She didn't, Neil."

"Powell has bad genes," he stated. "My brother said we have to r-remove the bloodline."

"I explained to Ellis that the serial-killer gene is a myth." No response.

"Neil, I'm so sorry for the pain James Ray Powell caused your family," Everleigh stated. "You have to know that if you try to continue along this path, Powell continues to win. He thrived on taking power from the women he raped and he's doing the same with you and Ellis. *He wins every time you hurt an innocent person.*"

Out the corner of her eye, she saw police officers and the SWAT team take their positions.

"Do you really want to keep giving your power to the man who took your mother from you?"

Neil didn't respond right away, but when he did, he said, "My brother told me that if you don't wanna be a victim, y-you hit first. He says that people only respect strength. Besides, t-this world ain't nothing but a cruel place filled with people who are evil. Like your f-father."

"I'd like to help you…if you'd let me."

"I don't need your kinda help."

"Neil, I don't believe you're like Ellis. I haven't met you, but I'm pretty sure you really don't want to hurt anyone. I understand that you look up to your brother."

"He tried to protect me. I o-owe him my life."

Neil sounded calmer now. Everleigh noticed that he wasn't stuttering as much.

"There's already been too much death. Please let the students leave the library."

"It's too late for us now."

"If you release the students and turn yourself in, this doesn't have to end in tragedy," she said.

"You say that, but I can see the police," Neil responded. "They want me dead."

"We don't want that at all. None of us. I want you to know that it's never too late to do what's right." Everleigh paused a moment, then said, "You and Ellis were so young when your mother died and unfortunately two innocent boys ended up in foster care, your basic needs stripped away—love, identity and security. When something like that happens, it becomes easier to express anger and blame the closest target. Neil, I'm sure you don't want to become like the very person you hate."

She heard a click then silence.

Everleigh turned to Declan and collapsed in his arms. "I pray I was able to get through to him."

Declan held her close. "The ball is in his court now."

He continued to be amazed by Everleigh. Her tone was caring and soothing and free of judgment. He truly hoped that Neil would give himself up, but he wasn't sure how the man would respond. He and his brother were ruthless in their killing. Men like that rarely went down without a fight.

Declan was grateful that Everleigh was safe and he intended to keep her that way. There was no way he was going to let her walk into that library. Rae needed her mother. But she wasn't the only one. He needed her, too.

The negotiator called again, but Neil didn't answer.

"The library doors are opening," someone said over the two-way radio.

Everleigh's eyes grew wet with unshed tears when the six students rushed out. "Thank You, God," she whispered.

After they ran out, the SWAT team entered the building.

Declan embraced Everleigh.

"I hope he'll give up without a fight," she said. Deep down, she prayed she was able to get through to Neil.

"Look," Declan uttered.

Everleigh released a sigh of relief when Neil was escorted out in handcuffs.

She was about to walk toward him, but Declan held her back. "Don't get too close…"

Everleigh and Neil made eye contact for a moment before he was placed in a cruiser.

"I looked into his eyes," she said. "He doesn't have the soul of a killer."

Relieved, Declan embraced her. "It's over. The Ragland brothers are in jail, and so is Wyle Gaines."

She couldn't be happier. They could finally put this behind them and focus on a future together.

"I need to speak to the supervisor in charge for a second," he told her.

"I think I'll go to my office. Just come get me when you're done."

"I won't be long."

Everleigh smiled at him. "I'm not going anywhere, so take your time."

TWENTY-ONE

Everleigh was about to enter through the doors of the social-sciences building when a tall figure of a man loomed in front of her, blocking her path. His face was partially shrouded by the black hoodie he was wearing. Something hit her, a memory of seeing someone in a hoodie watching her office... She'd thought it was Wyle. But...

"Where do you think you're going, Dr. Taylor?"

"Excuse me?"

Stunned, Everleigh glanced down at the gun in his hand. There were no other people around them. Everyone's attention was focused on the hostages and the police. "Who are you?"

"I'm Ellis and Neil's big brother."

She eyed him in confusion. "Olivia Ragland only had two sons."

"We have the same father. I was in a detention center when Olivia was murdered by your father. After that, I ended up in prison, so it took me years before I was able to find them after I got out. My brothers were abused physically and sexually by people who were supposed to be taking care of them."

"I'm really sorry that happened to them, but I'm not the one to blame—"

"Your parents *are*. Your mother's dead, and we can't get to your father." His face split into a grin. "But we have *you*."

Panic washed over Everleigh like a wave but she managed to keep her voice calm. *"Powell raped my mother."*

"I watched the way you handled Neil. I'm not lettin' you get inside my head, Dr. Taylor."

"Your brother was finally able to see the truth about this situation," she responded.

"He saw what you wanted him to see. Neil's always been the sensitive one. Afraid of his own shadow."

Everleigh tried to resist him as he practically dragged her toward a dark vehicle.

"You don't have to do this. You must know that the police will be looking for me."

"And they won't find you. Until it's too late."

She tried once again to pull her arm free.

He squeezed it tighter. "Don't try that again. I don't want to have to break that arm."

Everleigh could tell by the sinister expression on his face that he meant it.

At his SUV, he gave her a shove. *"Get in."*

She swung, clipping him in the chin.

He was quick in his reaction. "Feisty, I see. It won't bother me one bit to kill you right here." Pointing the gun at her head, he repeated his order. "I said, get inside."

He pulled a piece of wire from within the dash console and secured her hands together, then walked briskly around to the driver's side and got in.

Any hope of Declan coming to her rescue faded along with Everleigh's view of the campus as he drove them away.

Declan walked briskly toward the social-sciences building. He'd arranged to take tomorrow off because he was taking Everleigh back to Columbia. He knew she'd want to get back to Rae as quickly as she could.

"Professor Blanchet…"

"Hey—"

"Do you remember me? Aaron Edwards. Are you looking for your lady friend? Dr. Taylor?"

"I'm headed to her office right now."

"She's not there."

"What do you mean she's not there?" Declan demanded.

"I was in my car about to leave campus when I saw this guy forcing her into his SUV. It looked like he had a gun." He handed Declan a piece of paper. "Here's the license-plate number."

"How long ago?"

"About ten minutes ago. They were heading north."

"Thank you for this."

"Professor Blanchet, let me go with you," Aaron said. "I was military police and besides that, I can help you identify the SUV."

"C'mon."

They rushed to his car and drove in the direction the vehicle went. Declan hoped Everleigh's phone was still with her.

The most pressing question on his mind was who had kidnapped Everleigh. Both Ellis and Neil were in custody. So was Wyle Gaines.

Declan called a friend of his. "Hey, I need you to run a Maryland license plate for me."

When he got off the phone, he asked Aaron, "What brought you to campus tonight?"

"I came to talk to some students at the request of a friend," Aaron responded. "I've known her for almost ten years. Actually, she's the reason I chose to attend college in Charleston."

"I'm glad you were there."

His phone rang.

"The tags belong to a 2019 Honda Civic. They were reported stolen."

"What is the owner's name?"

"They belong to a Winston Powell."

One of the family members who had been murdered recently. "He's deceased. Whoever this perp is, he's connected to a string of murders."

"I hope you don't mind my asking, but what's going on?" Aaron asked. "I gathered that the guy arrested earlier was after Dr. Taylor. I heard something about a brother in jail."

"Yeah. The Ragland brothers blame Everleigh for their mother's death—something she had absolutely nothing to do with. There's a third man who's been stalking her, but he's in custody in South Carolina."

"And now there's a fourth player," Aaron said.

Declan nodded.

"How old were they when their mother died?"

"Young. Their father brought them home and they found her body."

"Where's Dad now?"

"No idea. He's been missing for a number of years."

"Maybe that's who this guy is," Aaron said. "The man I saw… He looked older, but I couldn't get a real good look at him because of his hoodie."

Declan stole a peek at him. "Hmm…it's worth investigating."

He called his friend back and said, "Hey, see if you can find any information on Ellison Ragland. Check all the databases. Send it to my phone."

"What is your name?" Everleigh asked.

"Romelle."

"Where are you taking me?" Everleigh asked.

"Somewhere where we can be alone."

"Why not just pull off to the side of the road and kill me now?"

He laughed. "You're still tryin' to get in my head. Ain't gonna happen, lady. You can relax because right now, you're worth more to me alive. If they want you back, they'll have to free my brothers."

"That's not going to happen. They won't release Ellis and Neil."

"It's either that or your little girl grows up without a mother. Think about everything that could happen to her without someone to protect her."

Everleigh raised her eyes upward and said a silent prayer. There was no one to help her. It was all up to God.

She refused to show him fear, so as calmly as she could manage, she said, "Romelle, you must know that this is not going to go the way you planned."

"Oh, it's gonna go exactly the way I want," he responded. "See, I ain't afraid of dying. But you—you have a daughter to think about. If you want her to stay safe, you will do exactly what I say." Romelle glanced over at her. "Folks like me and my brothers…we have to dispense our own justice. When Olivia died, you would've thought my pops would step up—he didn't. He ran away from his responsibility. When I got out of prison, I found him… He tried to tell me that they were better off without him. I shot him right then and there."

She gasped.

"Oh, he deserved it. He failed my little brothers. They don't know that I killed him. It's better for them to think that he's missing."

"It makes it easier for you to control them," she responded. "To get them to do what you want."

"This whole plan was my idea." He grinned at her, and the expression sickened her.

"But Wyle Gaines…" she began.

He laughed cruelly. "I heard from Olivia's landlord all about your mama. It's me who tracked her down. I was watching you for a while. I saw you turn Gaines down about the house. I got him talking about his troubles in that bar and then sent my little brothers over to hear all about it. I let Ellis and Neil think it was some kind of destiny, meeting Gaines. But it was my plan to take down Powell's family and end his bloodline. We even took out that pervert of a foster father. He died squealing like a pig…"

Everleigh prayed Declan was able to track her phone. But each mile marker they passed put more distance between them. She was going to have to do something.

Assessing her situation, she eyed the speedometer. They weren't wearing seat belts, and Romelle was driving above the speed limit. It was much too risky for her to try and jump out of the SUV, especially with her hands tied.

Her eyes strayed to the steering wheel.

God, if I do this, I'm going to really need Your help. I don't want to lose my life—I just want to stop this vehicle and Romelle. A crash would draw the police.

Everleigh moved with purpose. She reached over, grabbing the wheel with her bound hands.

"Wha—"

The car veered off the road as they struggled in the front seat. Romelle punched her in the chest, and the force sent her backward, toward the passenger side door.

They were headed toward a thicket of trees.

Everleigh didn't know if her idea had been such a smart one, but it was the only thing she could think of doing at the time. Her chest throbbed as she braced herself for impact.

The SUV connected with a huge tree.

She heard the grinding of metal and the shattering of glass. Everleigh caught a glimpse of Romelle's body being hurled forward into the windshield before falling back into the driver seat. The impact was a hard one.

Glass cut into her flesh, pain slicing through her face and arms as the edges of darkness closed in around her. She prayed once more, begging God to spare her life.

TWENTY-TWO

Everleigh opened her eyes with a start.

She was still inside the SUV.

Romelle wasn't moving. He looked unconscious.

Using her mouth, she worked to get the wire from around her hands. Once her left hand was free, her adrenaline kicked in; Everleigh slipped out of the vehicle and ran. She had no idea where she was or where she was going. She just knew she had to get away in case Romelle regained consciousness.

She took in a deep breath to clear her head as her anxiety level rose. Her face was on fire and she felt nauseous. Everleigh was so anxious to escape that she'd left her purse inside the vehicle. Her phone was inside.

"I'm not going back there," she whispered.

Everleigh took in her surroundings. The moon was out, but the sky was dark and ominous-looking. She swallowed her fear, trusting that God was true to His word. He was her protector and no harm would come to her.

Pain shot across her expression, compressing her features.

She saw the lights of a vehicle as it slowed and came to a stop. It wasn't the police. She feared that there could be others with Romelle. She didn't know how many people were helping Neil and Ellis, so she thought it best to remain out of sight.

Everleigh ran deeper into the wooded area.

In the distance, she saw two figures get out of the SUV and pressed herself against the tree. At one point, the SUV looked like Declan's, but he would've come alone. Tears filled her eyes in her disappointment.

Declan, where are you? I need you.

"That's the car over there," Aaron said.

Declan read the license tag, pulled off the road and parked his vehicle. He got out quickly. Panic rioted within his body as he prayed that Everleigh was fine. That she'd survived the accident.

I can't lose her now, Lord.

They cautiously approached the SUV. Declan had his gun drawn.

"There's someone inside," Aaron said.

Peering inside, he said, "It's the driver, but where's Everleigh?"

"Looks like she managed to get out of the vehicle. She's got to be somewhere in these woods."

"I need to find her quick," Declan said. "She could be injured. Stay with him."

He turned on his flashlight, searching the surroundings and calling out for her. "Everleigh!"

Nothing.

"It's me… Declan. If you can hear me, just follow my voice."

He walked deeper into the wooded area. "Everleigh, I'm here."

Declan heard a sound just ahead of him. He released the breath he'd been holding when the light from his flashlight landed on her.

His rushed to her side, embracing her. "She's alive," he yelled. "I found her."

"I was afraid I'd never see you and Rae again," Everleigh said before breaking down into sobs. "I was so scared."

Declan led her through the refuge of trees. When they approached the SUV, Declan said, "This is Aaron. He'll walk you to the car. I want to make sure your kidnapper doesn't try to escape."

"No," Everleigh responded, tears running down her face. "We should go. Let's just get out of here," she pleaded. "Before he manages to wake up."

He walked back over to the wrecked SUV. "From the looks of it, he's not going anywhere. The police are on the way—I intend to make sure this guy goes from the hospital straight to the jail."

The blaring of police sirens broke up the silence.

Everleigh bent over as she tried to quiet her heavy breathing.

Declan wrapped his arm around her waist. "Are you okay? Are you in any pain?"

"Just got a little out of breath. I'll be fine."

A police car came into view.

"What is his connection to the brothers?" Declan asked.

"He's their half-brother," Everleigh responded. "His name is Romelle. Apparently, he was locked up when they were placed in a group home. How did you know where to find me? Were you able to track my phone?"

"Aaron happened to be sitting in his car and saw everything."

Everleigh turned toward him. "I'm so grateful you were there. Thank you for being so diligent."

"I'm glad I was able to help," Aaron replied. "I wanted to intervene when I first realized what was going on, but then I saw the gun."

"Wait… I've seen you before. On campus."

He nodded. "The day I met with Professor Blanchet. I was leaving his office and you were coming to see him."

"You have good instincts," Declan said. "I'm looking forward to having you in my class."

"I'm just glad we were able to get Professor Taylor back. It doesn't always turn out this way."

"I feel very fortunate," Everleigh responded. "Right now, all I want to do is see my daughter."

"After they check you out in the hospital, I'll take you to her," Declan said.

"I told you that I'm fine."

"It's dark but I can see that you have some bruising on your face as well as cuts. You're bleeding."

Declan, Everleigh and Aaron watched as Romelle was taken out of the SUV and loaded into an ambulance. A police officer walked over to speak with Everleigh.

When they were given the okay to leave, Declan said, "They're all in custody now."

"But it's not over yet," Everleigh responded. "What if Romelle manages to escape the hospital?"

"He won't," Declan assured her. "He's got some head trauma and might need surgery. But after he's out of the woods, he'll be handcuffed to the bed."

Declan held open the passenger-side door.

Everleigh slid inside. The only thing on her mind in this moment was seeing her daughter. She couldn't wait to hold Rae in her arms.

"Where are we heading?" she asked.

"The hospital."

"I don't want to do that."

"Everleigh, you need to be checked out," he said. "Then I'll take you to your daughter."

When they arrived to the emergency entrance, Aaron

said, "My friend's coming to pick me up. I'll wait out here until she comes."

Declan shook his hand. "Thank you for everything."

"I'm glad it turned out this way."

After Everleigh was registered and given a room, Declan was allowed to join her.

"I just got off the phone with Sherri. She wants you to know that the girls are having a ball together. I told her we'd be there sometime tomorrow."

"Thanks, Declan," Everleigh responded. "I don't want her worrying about me." She shifted her position on the bed. "I really hope they don't try to keep me. I feel fine."

"You're lying," he said. "You have some cuts that need to be looked at, but not only that...you're grimacing every now and then. I can see that you're in pain."

Shortly, a doctor came in and examined her. "Mrs. Taylor, you've got glass in the cut on your forehead," the doctor said. "I'm going to remove it and put a bandage on you."

She turned her head to one side, eyes closed. "My head hurts and my chest. He punched me when I grabbed the steering wheel."

After an examination, the doctor didn't see any signs of external bleeding other than her head. He ordered a battery of tests to determine if she'd sustained any internal damage.

"Why is this taking so long," Everleigh complained.

Declan handed her his phone so that she could call and talk to Rae. He hoped it would help to calm her some.

"Hey, sweetie."

"Mama, where are you?"

"I had to take care of something at the university. I had a little car accident. I'm fine, so there's no need to worry."

"Did you get hurt?"

"A few cuts and scratches," Everleigh responded. "But I should be there tomorrow. Okay? Mr. Declan is with me."

"Okay. I'll see you soon, Mama."

"That went much better than I thought it would," Everleigh said as she handed the phone back to Declan. "I don't know why, but I feel a little disappointed."

"I can assure you that little girl misses you."

A nurse walked into the room, putting a pause in their conversation.

When she left, Everleigh said, "Freedom first thing in the morning…"

He chuckled. "I'll be here early to pick you up."

Declan sent up a prayer of thanksgiving. The worst was over for now. When the Ragland brothers went to trial, Everleigh's secret would be exposed, but she wouldn't have to face it alone. He would stand beside her.

"I'm glad to finally leave this hospital," Everleigh said the next morning as they walked through the parking lot to the car. "I can't wait to put my arms around Rae. I wasn't sure I'd ever see her again."

"You risked your life trying to take the wheel like that," Declan said when they were on the road. "That accident could've ended up being much worse."

"I know, but I had to do something," she responded. "If I hadn't, there's no telling how this would've turned out."

"I'm glad I found you when I did."

"Me, too," she murmured. Staring out the passenger-side window, Everleigh asked, "Are we heading to Columbia?"

He nodded.

"Good."

"I had no idea there was another brother. We thought

that maybe it was Ellison Ragland, their father, who kidnapped you."

"I can understand why," she murmured.

"Especially since Ellison has been missing for years."

Gently rubbing her temple with her right hand, she said, "We had no way of knowing there was a half-brother on their father's side. Romelle said that killing off Powell's bloodline was *his* idea. You should've heard him. He was proud of it. He said something else—he told me that he killed his father because he'd failed Neil and Ellis. That's why nothing's come up on Ellison."

"As soon as he recovers, the brothers will be reunited in jail," Declan stated. "Romelle can spend the rest of his life trying to protect them in prison."

"I got the distinct impression that Romelle was always the one in charge. Ellis had the most rage. Neil seemed on the fence, but he's loyal to his brothers."

"This explains why the victims were killed in different ways," Declan said. "I thought it was because the perp was deliberately trying to hide the connection between the crimes. I'm thinking now that Ellis was the one who bludgeoned his victims. Romelle had a gun so he probably shot his victims. I'm not sure Neil killed anyone. He was probably more of a witness than anything."

"Romelle intended to use me to try and get his brothers out of jail," Everleigh said. "But he still intended to kill me. Just in the short time I was with him, I could tell he's a sociopath."

"While you were being examined, I found out that Romelle was arrested for killing another teen when he was fourteen," Declan said. "He's been in and out of trouble from the time he was eleven years old."

"Eleven? What on earth did he do at eleven?"

"He was killing animals."

Everleigh shook her head sadly. "Then he killed his own father and manipulated his half-brothers into murder. He created monsters."

The heaviness of sleep began to overtake her. "I'm going to take a quick nap for a half hour," she thought, succumbing to the need for rest.

When Everleigh woke up, Declan was turning on Lakeshore. She could hardly contain her joy. She couldn't wait to see her daughter.

When they walked into the house, Rae rushed to her side.

"Mama, you have a boo-boo on your head."

She wrapped her arms around her. "I'm fine. I promise."

"I was a good girl. Ask Miss Sherri."

"I'm so proud of you, sweetie."

"Were you brave at the hospital?" Rae asked.

Everleigh glanced over at Declan. "What would you say?"

"She was very brave," he replied.

"Mama, I'm proud of you," Rae said.

Everleigh spent the rest of her evening with her daughter until the little girl went to sleep.

She heard someone in the kitchen and went to investigate.

"I'm sorry. Did I wake you?" Declan asked. "I was in the mood for a piece of pie and some milk."

Everleigh sat down across from him at the table. "I wasn't sleeping. I thought you'd left already and I heard a noise."

Declan reached over and took her hand in his own. "How are you feeling?"

"A bit antsy," she responded. "Shaken…even a little bit scared… Okay, a lot scared, even though I know it's over."

He smiled. "That's normal."

"It's hard to stop thinking of what could've happened... you know, the worst-case scenarios."

Declan gave her a reassuring smile. "It may take a day or two but those feelings will go away." He pointed to the sweet-potato pie. "You should have a slice of this. It's delicious."

"It does look good."

Declan cut her a slice and placed it on a plate. "What would you like to drink?"

"Hot chocolate," Everleigh responded. "My mom used to make me a cup whenever I was down or felt afraid."

"Then I'll make you some."

"I don't know what I'd do without you, Declan," she said. "You've been a wonderful friend to me. You also kept your promise. You said you'd keep us safe and you did just that."

"Just so you know, I don't consider my job officially over until after Ellis, Neil and Romelle are tucked away in prison for good."

Everleigh took a sip of her hot chocolate. "What happens after that?" she asked. "We go back to a friendly wave and a nod."

"You can't get rid of me that easily," Declan responded with a chuckle. "I hope we will remain friends or something more..."

"I'd like that. I'd really like that. Since you're here, would you like to watch a movie or we could just talk," Everleigh said.

"If you're not too tired."

She finished off her pie. "Declan, can I ask you a very personal question?"

"Sure."

"Why haven't you gotten married?"

"I always thought I'd be married by now, but I guess it

just wasn't meant to be," he responded. "What about you? Do you think you'll ever remarry?"

"Just a few short weeks ago, I wasn't sure I ever would," Everleigh said. "But I really loved being married and I don't want Rae to grow up alone. I'd like to have more children."

"I'm happy to hear this because I'd love to take you on a real date. Whenever you're ready for something like that."

"I want to be honest with you, Declan. I'm very attracted to you, but the fact that you worked in law enforcement initially turned me off. My late husband was a firefighter. He died on the job. I didn't want to put Rae through another loss like that. Then I realized I was being irrational. I was angry with God because I wanted Him to protect Britt, and when he died, I felt that God failed me."

"Do you still feel that way?"

"I don't," Everleigh responded. "God has shown me in so many ways that He is who He says He is. He protected me when I was with Romelle. Crashing the car was risky and stupid, but God didn't let me die. I can't explain it—I just know He was with me. I was protected."

"It's funny you should bring my career up," he said, a crooked grin on his face. "I get so much out of teaching, and working with Aaron to get you home safely convinced me what I want to do. The faculty offered me a full-time teaching position and I've decided to take them up on it."

"You're leaving the police department?"

Declan nodded. "I'm really enjoying teaching. However, I'll still consult for them whenever needed."

Everleigh broke into a grin.

"Things just got interesting, don't you think?"

"Definitely," she responded.

TWENTY-THREE

Everleigh sat on a bench outside of the social-services building, waiting for Declan's class to end. It felt good being on campus and teaching in-person. Most of her classes were in-person this semester, with one virtual class in the mix.

He strolled out of the building at twelve noon. Declan lowered himself carefully onto the bench beside her. "I like seeing your beautiful face back here on school grounds."

"I'm thrilled to be back, all things considered," she responded. "Rae's very happy being back at school with her kindergarten class."

"I was just about to ask about her."

"She's good. Oh, this is for you." Everleigh handed him a folded piece of paper. "Rae drew a picture for you."

"It's the three of us together."

She nodded. "Rae had a lot of fun at your sister's house. *With you.* She really likes you, Declan."

"I'm crazy about that little girl and her mother."

He planted a quick kiss on her lips, then said, "What do you think about dinner and a play?" he inquired. "This Saturday."

Excitement floated through her. "Are you talking about the new DeSantis play?"

"Yes," Declan responded.

"Oh, I'd love that," Everleigh exclaimed. "I've been wanting to see it, but I didn't relish going alone."

"I have tickets. I bought them with the intent to take my sister, but then her job sent her abroad."

"I'm excited."

"I can tell," Declan said with a chuckle.

"I don't know about you, but I'm hungry," she stated, holding up a lunch bag. "I made an extra sandwich."

Everleigh took a bite of her sandwich, but her eyes never left Declan's face as he swiped her pickle to add to his own sandwich.

"You love pickles, I see."

He grinned. "I do. I usually order extra pickles."

"I'll keep that in mind."

She retrieved a bag of potato chips. "I have another bag if you want it."

Declan gave a slight nod as he wiped his mouth on the paper napkin.

"I just got a news alert," Everleigh said while looking at her phone. "James Ray Powell is dead. Apparently, he had cancer."

Declan checked his phone. "I got a notification, too."

They sat in silence for a moment before Everleigh said, "I don't feel anything but relief. I'm not happy that he's dead or anything, but I can't deny that I'm relieved he won't ever know about me or Rae. I feel like I can finally close that door permanently."

"There's still four people out there who know about this."

"I'm not worried about Wyle Gaines. He has enough to deal with now that his past is catching up to him. And if he decides to tell anyone about me, he doesn't have any proof. As for the Ragland brothers—all three of them—they don't have any proof, either. There's nothing for them to gain in telling the world. Powell's dead. He was my biggest concern."

"They all have credibility issues for sure."

"I'm not worried," Everleigh said. "None of them have any power over me."

James Ray Powell was laid to rest in the prison cemetery two days later. Nobody had come forward to claim his remains. The world would breathe a collective sigh of relief now that he was gone, Everleigh included. For the first time since her nightmare started, the future looked promising once again.

Even if Powell hadn't died, she'd already refused to allow the sins of her father to weigh her down. There were still some emotions and processes she had to go through. She'd experienced a period of denial when her mother first told her about him, then rode the pendulum of shock and anger. But now she was in the acceptance phase. Powell's actions were not a reflection of herself or Rae.

Everleigh stood in front of the full-length mirror, checking her reflection. She'd chosen a velvet mid-length dress in burgundy with matching suede boots for her date with Declan.

Although the past two years had been filled with challenges, she was finally ready for her future.

EPILOGUE

One year later

"This place is uncomplicated living at its best," Everleigh said. "I almost hate going back to Charleston tomorrow."

Declan took her hand in his as they walked the trail around the lake. "So you really like it here in Columbia?"

She looked over at him. "I love it here."

"I guess we should get back to the house," he said. "I promised Rae I'd help her with reading."

"Don't let her manipulate you into reading to her when it's her turn to read out loud."

He grinned. "I won't."

As soon as they walked into the house, they were met by Rae, who said, "Mama, we found this while we were taking down the Christmas tree. It's for you." She held up a gift-wrapped box.

Everleigh took it from her. "Who is it from?"

"Oh, yeah… I forgot all about that one," Declan said.

"Open it, Mama."

"Okay," she murmured. Everleigh couldn't begin to guess what it could be—the box was rectangular in shape. It could be a shirt…anything.

She tore the wrapping away.

Inside that box was a beautiful hand-carved jewelry

box—it was one she'd seen in a boutique downtown. Declan had pointed it out to her, but never indicated he'd purchased it.

His sister Marguerite, Remy, Sherri and the girls were gathered around her, admiring the gift.

Everleigh turned to thank Declan and found him on bended knee.

"That jewelry box is actually one of two gifts. Here is the second one," he said, opening the black velvet box to reveal a stunning engagement ring.

"Declan…"

"Will you do me the honor of becoming my wife?"

Tears of joy sprang in Everleigh's eyes. "Yes. Yes. *Yes.*"

Rae clapped her hands in glee. "I'm getting another daddy."

Everleigh fell into Declan's embrace.

"Oh, my goodness," she murmured. "We're really doing this. We're getting married."

"Yeah, we are. I'm ready to spend the rest of my life with you."

She held her hand out, admiring the ring.

"Congratulations," Marguerite said. "I've always wanted a sister."

"Now you really are part of the family!" Sherri said.

Everleigh smiled. "Same here."

Remy brought out a bottle of non-alcoholic Champagne for the adults and apple juice for Rae and Halle. "It's time for a toast."

After each of them had a flute, Remy said, "Uncle, I'm so happy for you, Everleigh and Rae. From the moment Sherri and I saw the three of you together, we knew… we just sensed that your worlds would eventually become one. Cheers."

They took a sip.

She reached for Declan's hand, lacing her fingers with his. "I never really imagined that I'd feel this way again—truly excited about what the future holds. I know that there will always be challenges, but I'm glad I don't have to face them alone."

Declan looked down at their linked hands. "We will meet life head-on…together."

"Yay… Rae's my sister now," Halle said, sparking laughter from everyone in the room.

Declan flashed her a grin. "Let's just go with it for tonight."

Everleigh nodded in agreement. This was the start of a new life together.

* * * * *